Yellow City
Stories

Yellow City
Stories

Erika Tanaka

MOONHAW

ISBN: 979-8-9888307-0-2

Cover art by Sabina Kencana
Book design by Manuel Quintana
Author photo by Logan Power
Epigram from Kandinsky, Wassily, and Michael Sadleir. *Concerning the Spiritual in Art*. IAP, 2009.

Printed and bound in the USA
First printing September 2023

Published by Moonhaw Press
2368 Route 214
Lanesville, NY

moonhaw.com

For Obachama

Yellow, if steadily gazed at in any geometrical form, has a disturbing influence, and reveals in the color an insistent, aggressive character.

Kandinsky

Table of Contents

Sixth Avenue Sangha

ON HER NEW SPIRITUAL BIRTHDAY, Dawn Williams felt like a little girl all in white again, reluctant to make her First Communion. Her trepidation was as genuine as any cradle Catholic tottering toward the rail, albeit no crucifix was in sight. Her sentimentalism was overkill. Dawn was not Catholic; she was raised quasi-Protestant and married a disillusioned Catholic.

Her initiation took place at eight past one in the afternoon, two days after Buddha's birthday (or mud season in the Himalayas). In Manhattan, it was that stunted time of year when the super had switched off the heat for the whole building but was yet to have the air conditioners serviced. For almost two weeks, inner and outer temperatures had coexisted—even on the subway. Weather ambiguity plus humidity amplified neuroses, and many New Yorkers capitalized on the increased anxiety of styleless Americans who did not know how to dress for such unnatural equilibrium. Dawn had conquered this problem of micro-seasons feted by fashion people as "the transition" in her early forties. Now just the other side of fifty, she could focus on conquering the real stuff: karma and liberation.

Like Mary, the religious attachment she was getting ready to leave behind, Dawn's primary identity was that of an ordinary wife and mother. She reminded herself of this as she eyed the Asian-style altar through the open sliding doors. *I am a mother to a young woman; they are not the enemy.* The intrusive thought, jealousy, began when she entered the Zendo and came face-to-face with an attractive blond intern who helped her robe up for the ceremony.

The twenty-something was wearing a lilac linen jumpsuit with the impossible air of thrifting. The fabric flowed along the supple lines of her stem-like body, much like fresh snow clings to a spectacular fall line. Dawn side-eyed the intern all morning when she should have focused on her upcoming salvation. She fully invested in comparing the girl's appearance to herself at that age, x-raying for physical flaws that could indicate moral failing.

The intern kept quiet as she helped Dawn fork her elbows into her brand-new koromo robe (which she'd ordered from an Etsy shop run by someone in Russia called "Anton"). The shop boasted five stars and also sold ninja suits. When it arrived, Dawn had put it on and then sent a silly selfie to her daughter, who had sent back crying-laughing-face emojis before accusing her of raiding Baby Yoda's closet.

Dawn had been allergic to contemplation all her life, obsessively avoiding plastic and talking about feelings, and sleeping well. She was becoming a formal Zen student not because of emotion but to save her marriage.

A small, worn hanshō and mallet hung beside the sliding rice paper doors. When it was time to begin, the intern in the lilac jumpsuit took it up tepidly and batted it against itself. The other two more experienced interns glared at her. To be asked by one of the senseis to hit the hanshō was a huge honor, and they all vied for it.

Whenever the primitive wood bell was struck, the 108 hand-folded orizuru garlanding the doorway trembled. The throats of one thousand paper cranes were pierced by a Singer sewing needle before being strung up on a red thread and presented by the sangha to their senseis on the occasion of their marriage, which garnered a lovely write-up in *The Times*. Naturally, no one in the sangha folded a thing. The paper cranes had been made in China and purchased in Chinatown. Dawn had gone downtown with Denise, the sangha's party planner, only to witness this White woman from Long Island make drama by demanding a discount in the name of Buddhist solidarity.

"But these are for our senseis!"

Denise, a forty-something environmental attorney, deployed her most persuasive spiritual fellowship language, but the confounded Burmese shopkeeper had refused to budge. He simply shook his head when the White lawyer argued with him about "benevolence" and "merit." Growing more and more frustrated with her literal interpretation of his spiritual law, the shopkeeper had retorted, "No, no, no, no, no. Buddha no discount," before reiterating the price.

The women had left Chinatown paying full price for their senseis' cranes, plus tax. Denise, naturally, took this to mean the shopkeeper didn't understand English (let alone enlightenment!). It never occurred to her that there had been no miscommunication. Instead, the lawyer focused on how she thought it was a shame that Maoists had destroyed all of China's ancient religion and culture and complained as much out loud to Dawn in the Uber back uptown.

"The West may be shit for many reasons, but at least we rescued heaps of Eastern wisdom that would have otherwise been caught up in all that colonial madness. So sad, isn't it? Chinese people invented meditation, but then they forgot all about it."

Dawn knew from all the reading she was doing in preparation for her jukai that this was not precisely true, but the cranes were beyond charming, so she let the hectic dialectic fade away naturally. The unpleasant interaction with the undharmaic shopkeeper evaporated from both women's memories as soon as the newlywed sensei were delighted with their photogenic paper gifts.

Week in, week out, beneath the shelter of 216 trembling wings, the Sixth Avenue Sangha chanted the *Heart Sūtra* in English and paid homage to every manifestation of Buddha, dharma, and sangha—in all ten directions. They honored the teachers of their lineage, the bodhisattva succession, and their ancestors. Amid the endless churn of chanting, sitting, and kinhin, no one ever noticed how all this contemplative brouhaha disturbed the stillness of the paper birds strung up on the thin red line above the door.

When she'd first decided to do it, she thought it would be like eating a sandwich, but so far, her initiation ceremony was going rather romantically. In the fullness of her untamed anxiety, Dawn stood alone and freshly bathed in the center of the shrine room. Her body put out the subtle scent of Fifth Avenue department store foyers. Diffused luxury with an omnipresent hint of Christmas blended with a seductive foreign (usually French) name. Dawn's immaculate honey-blond blow-out waved water-like around the bony coastline of her upper body. Freshly lowlighted to bring out her natural amber, its volume has been tactfully coiffed to look like it had dried due to a coastal wind moving through it. These days, women funneled effort into making themselves look like all effort was dead. Among the young, the goal was to present the appearance of no effort to augment the already perfect (cheekbones, waist, ass, etc.). Among the less young, appearing to arrest time's march through the power of one's positivity, self-awareness, and superior wellness skills was the supreme target. Unfortunately, despite the best efforts of her private yoga instructor, Dawn's collarbones still curled forward. Slightly concave, the beginning of a hunchback glimpsable beneath her silk chemise haunted her like the crucible of intimate relationships. Besides time's slight impress upon her shoulders, which could not be filtered away, the rest of her middle-age defects had been masterfully mollified for this special day. With her look dialed in, she could relax and synergize with her current container, the shrine room occupying the sixth floor of a nondescript but high-rent postwar building where Sixth Avenue and 21st Street met.

As the neighborhood shapeshifted, the building and its tenants attempted repeated, quietly upward design drift—for instance, the lobby. The tiny chamber was desperately restored with marigold marble strips that kaleidoscoped with mustard shades and anise lit by aggressive Art Deco sconces. Dawn *adored* the lobby the moment her rugged boots, which had never stepped in mud, first touched the yellowish marble. When she came for the after-work evening sits in the summer months, luminous paleness streamed into the lobby and mixed with its surroundings. Bathed in this Corsican light, the hard-earned creases on the mountain ranges of her face appeared as if lasered away by some expert surgeon. *This place is a portal*, she thought. In time, she fervently believed meditation would render her fatal flaws as a woman invisible. *Mindfulness is a more effective antidote than any $600 serum.*

After waiting for the sangha to file in (an interminable eternity), the gong was finally struck, and Dawn's jukai began. They started with the main event: the prescription of the sixteen bodhisattva vows, which meant that the monks recited many words in Japanese.

Boo, Soo, Moo, Roo, Kooo, Too!

Dawn did not know this strange language beyond the sushi menu basics but found it easy to follow along. First, she promised infinity to allow it to shape her like water shapes the rock. Dawn's mind drifted as the priests continued chanting—no different than when she was sitting in a pew. She visualized hanging out with the ancient Buddhas on Mount Izumi Katsuragi's bald peak and ancient yogis, who om'd themselves out of existence deep in some Himalayan cave.

"Dawn-san!" Sensei Kyodo, the bearded British monk, touched her shoulder gently to bring her back to the present moment. "It is time for your vows."

With great solemnity, Dawn took out her phone. She'd jotted the vows down only yesterday using the Notes app during her morning commute.

"Like in the traditional Western marriage ceremony, this part is the most important because it comes from you," cautioned the Kentish monk in their last pre-ceremony dokusan. His accent was broad and rolling. It constantly distracted her. "They define how you promise to live your life, which is unique to you and your journey, nobody else's."

Dawn worried that this vulnerable moment would overcome her with worthlessness, but nothing like that happened. She breezed through it.

Next, the two monks called upon her to confess her ancient and twisted karma before the sangha, including her husband, John. Dawn's mouth opened, and her historical neuroses charged like bats hibernating for years in a long-abandoned barn. Beginningless greed, hate, delusion, the "this person is crazy, that person is my enemy," she let it all hang out.

"In my twenties, I lied to my parents about a boy I was seeing and madly in love with," she confessed. "It was the sixties, and he was Black. I regularly went to church stoned in middle school and took communion high. Then, one time, in third grade, I shoplifted …"

Another touch on the concave shoulder from the molasses-tongued monk told her: *That's enough. We get it. You don't have to tell us every "bad" thing you've ever done.*

Dawn felt ashamed of her shame and immediately curtailed her confession. Proceeding to the next section of the ceremony, forty-eight times, she vowed and bowed. The statue of Avalokiteshvara on the altar swished its skirts compassionately at her. Still, Dawn felt judged as all thirty-odd sangha members answered her sincere requests to join their ancient order by taking photos of her (but mostly the monks) on their phones. The elders filmed shakily while the younger ones live-streamed, all the while ritualistically invoking the presence of all enlightened beings. All were thus awake and actively participating, except for John, Dawn's husband, who looked like he might shatter into ten thousand pieces at any moment.

Sensei Kyodo yawned, and the other monk saw it and gave him a disapproving yet still loving look.

Had John not threatened to divorce her unless they quit therapy to develop a shared spiritual practice, Dawn would never have known anything about Zen Buddhism and D. T. Suzuki besides that she *adored* the polypropylene stacking boxes at Muji. There was something inordinately soothing about so much see-through compartmentalization. But she *had* gone with her husband to learn zazen, and something in her had eventually begun to feel like one of those modular plastic boxes. Great for storing not only files, but also items such as newspapers and magazines.

After weeks of meditating, she found that she sat differently on the subway. She noticed things, like a tender moment between a homeless subway artist and a child admiring his work or octogenarian birders in Central Park noticing the birds. When she reported as much to John over poached eggs and avocado toast after a half-day Sunday sit, his eyes lit up in a way that she'd almost remembered what it had felt like to fall in love with him.

"You should take jukai," he beamed. "Ask them."

"Kneel, Dawn-san."

Time for the revelation of Dawn's dharma name. The cushion mistress with curly red hair toted out the cushion and painstakingly placed it on the floor before Dawn. The bell sounded, and the sangha member (who'd rung it a little too forcefully) showed terror in her eyes.

Dawn settled onto hollow kneecaps. *Can they hear me creaking?*

Sensei Ashita-En, the Midwestern teacher with no beard, read from a rice paper scroll: "When you give up attachments, you are free. You are Buddha."

Sensei Ashita-En then signaled to Sensei Kyodo to reach for the rakusu, which was folded and reverent like a flag on a soldier's coffin on the low Japanese table before the priests. It had waited, unnoticed till now, before the altar. This was the moment Dawn had long been waiting for—to read what her teachers had written on the back of her sacred, ancient bib. How appropriate for a feminist to be given a new bib upon rebirth! A machine-washable reminder to clean up after and mommy one's self. The new Zen name chosen for her was supposed to account for qualities she already had and those she needed to develop. Dawn had waited patiently for almost half a century to know her essence, humanity, and soul. Now, at last, she was to be revealed to herself.

Someone lit Kusa grass and lowered the smoldering tip of bound twigs into a ceramic cup of Evian. Sensei Kyodo used the little charred bushel as an aspergillum, incensing first himself, then the other priest, then each of the thirty sangha members with knees crooked on either side of their buckwheat pads. Sensei Kyodo brushed Dawn's forehead and lips.

"I am purifying your mouth."

Somewhere, Dawn knew, John was also waiting on his knees. Poor, holy man! Like Lazarus at the gate, he ached from long years of longing to bring her across before he brought himself. For years, he'd been striving to contrive of his wife as an independent being and not measure their marriage in false, documented equivalences like licenses, children birthed (or stillborn), and anniversary candles blown out. For a man to meet his wife as a fellow being meant that her purification could also be his. Interconnectedness was to be found everywhere, so why not in the admixture of kuso-water, sweat, and other bodily secretions married men prefer to speak about only privately? God himself had joined them in marriage. One flesh, two souls (or was it the other way around?). Her path was also his, and vice versa. Right? He believed this, honestly, even though their marriage had almost imploded three times sixteen times. Now that they had stopped trying to save it by saving each other, he was sure *a new opportunity could be recognized*. All these years later, they were still sharing an apartment and a life but no longer sharing a soul.

Early on in her conversion process, Sensei Ashita-End cryptically said, "You might have to wait for the right conditions to arise."

Only today did Dawn finally understand what the koan meant. She'd always been a good Episcopalian girl. Then a good Episcopalian girl married to a great Catholic man with whom she raised her daughter to identify as "nothing." Becoming a Zen Buddhist would not change anything; it would strengthen everything. How long did she squat in her mental filth, examining her psychic propensities toward self-annihilation? From the bottomless reserve of hidden inner resources, Dawn mined out of herself a quality she'd never known she possessed. That quality enshrined by therapists as "resilience" was experienced by her as a kind of terracotta earthiness—solid yet porous with the winds of despair whipping around it, howling and howling.

For months, Dawn had sat and sat in preparation for jukai. She'd sat in the early hours; she'd sat in the late hours. She'd sat in the lost hours that bled in between while her husband snored on the far side of their bed with separate sleep numbers. She did this every day for months, unwittingly unwilling to will until the desire for will itself was revealed to her as a transient impulse, nothing more. When her sitting was done, she'd drift into the guest bathroom, turn

16

on the shower without stepping inside, stand naked in front of the mirror, and bow to everyone she loved, hated, and feared.

Bow to the Buddhas in the ten directions! To your dead mother, dying father, living husband, and forsaken children! Bow to your boss! Bow to your manicurist! Bow to the frat boy who put drugs in your drink, ripped off your jeans, and pushed himself inside you when you were just seventeen! Bow to the bastard who married you! Bow and vow, dammit, bow and vow.

Sensei Kyodo pressed the rakusu into Dawn's clear-manicured hands, murmuring something sacred before regaling her with his signature Santa Claus smile. But Dawn did not hear the sacred syllables because her mind was, again, hidden in her thoughts.

She panicked when the realization of what had happened (or not happened) dawned on her. How could she miss *the* seminal moment of her initiation ceremony? She'd missed her teacher announcing her brand-new timeless name! A student could not ask her teacher to repeat himself. The masters of old would have sliced off the wrist of such an arrogant disciple and fed it to the foxes. She had no choice but to surrender to not knowing who she was yet again. Feeling annoyed and itchy behind her left knee, Dawn accepted her new spiritual name without knowing what it was. She was forced to pretend that she knew and already loved her dharma name more than the one her mother told the priest to give her more than half a century ago.

Meanwhile, Sensei Ashita-En was still preaching: "To love even the confusion, discouragement, and fixed views …"

The room was growing tired, which was not lost on the senseis, who knew their temple business must maintain good "energy flow." Sensei Kyodo rose and trod over to Dawn like he was walking across a field of diamonds. He gently placed the rakusu she sewed for herself atop her head. It fell off. He placed it again. Again, it fell off.

"Your hair is too shiny!" he giggled.

Dawn's impatience amplified. She snatched the bib and balanced it atop her skull. It hovered for a moment before sliding off again. Sensei Kyodo grabbed it and garlanded her in resignation.

"Now, dear one," he said, "go and stand on the chair. Someone give her a hand, please?"

The sangha wanted to be seen as obliging, but their legs were fast asleep after almost an hour of sitting. Six women leaped to the task. Unable to climb on furniture in two-toed tabi, Dawn was grateful for their help. When she was installed on the chair, eye to eye with Avalokiteshvara, the two priests led the following chant: "Buddha recognizes Buddha. Buddha bows to Buddha."

One at a time, the teachers approached Dawn towering unworthily on the rickety dining chair. They chanted and bowed. After them, the first sangha member stepped up, chanted, and bowed: "Buddha recognizes Buddha. Buddha bows to Buddha," then, the second, "Buddha recognizes Buddha. Buddha bows to Buddha," the third, "Buddha recognizes Buddha. Buddha bows to Buddha," and so on.

Dawn bowed back to everyone who bowed to her, conscious of the bottom of her feet lightly touching the wood of the seat through her stiff new tabi.

Frankincense fired on the altar. Each face was familiar to her, surprisingly dear. Tenderness spread inside her like a rash. Curiously, there was no judging of any kind. Only bow after bow, consecutive, never-ending.

At the paternal urging of Sensei Kyodo during a bathroom break, the lilac-clad intern took her place in line to bless and be blessed by Dawn. Older sangha members dangling from the chairs set out for those too stiff to sit cross-legged on the floor enviously watched this swan swim into the Zendo and settle quietly at the back. Dawn couldn't blame them. She was supple, beautiful, and settled early on her dharmic path— hating her was easy. *Surely, she'll get enlightened long before anyone else in the room.* It wasn't fair. The lilac-clad intern was precisely the kind of pretty young thing John liked to wedge in the void between them. Exactly the kind of pretty young thing she'd been when they'd first met when he did not yet need to distance himself from her.

The intern presented herself before Dawn, high on her chair, pressed her palms together, and bowed without lowering the plane of her forehead.

"Buddha recognizes Buddha. Buddha bows to Buddha."

Bow, bitch! To the lovely, hateful intern, Dawn bowed deeper than she had to anyone else, even the senseis. The girl, utterly oblivious to the eyes of the room devouring her form, nervously took her leave. She shuffled off to the back of the Zendo, uncertain what to do with her hands now.

Then, it was John's turn. Dawn had forgotten he was even there until some idea of husband suddenly stood before her. She felt him as she always did when he crept in beside her, thinking she was asleep when she was not. He was neither beside, away from, nor inside her (as he had been for most of their marriage). For years, her husband's presence had been its own practice.

He took his palms from the pockets of the Dockers she ordered online for him and squeezed them together in honor of her life as the life of Buddha. Her tabi itched between the two biggest toes. *Where isn't delusion?* Not in the deli, whose cold cuts she no longer procured for herself or her family because the precept of not-killing included all sentient beings. Not in the reformulation of *how* she scrubbed the bathtub or spoke harshly to her child, her coworkers, the nurses who tended to her senile father, her accountant, her attorney. *What is the opposite of killing, stealing, and sexual misconduct? Giving? Saving a life?*

Dawn's husband stared up at her. He had not stared at her like this before, ever. Not when he folded her hands in hers when Father Brian had asked him, "Do you take?" Not on their honeymoon in a gossamer tent on the beach when they visited the Theravadins in tangerine. Not at the very moment when he had collapsed out of her in a way that she just knew they'd conceived their first child. Not when he'd entered the room at Beth Israel and squeezed her hand when the doctor announced they had lost that child. Not when she'd successfully carried their only living offspring to term, and the bundle was placed, peach and pinched, into her arms. Not at her mother's funeral. At his sister's wake. At Maya's graduation from Brearley, from Cornell.

John recited slowly, pronouncing each syllable with a deliberateness that Dawn wished he would bring to the *Heart Sūtra*, the Four Vows, bidding their daughter goodnight or wishing his wife well for her day. When he said, "Buddha recognizes Buddha. Buddha bows to Buddha," all hurt vanished from his voice.

She knew he was pleased with himself when it was done from how he trotted off with short, fast steps to the southwest corner of the shrine room. There, he immediately commenced sobbing. Sensei Ashita-En scurried over to enfold the crying disciple inside the warm cove of his brown master's robe. For all the sangha to see, Dawn's husband wept his threefold sufferings on the day of *her* initiation.

A bonus practitioner stepped before her while her husband wept in the sensei's arms. Dawn had been so focused on the girl in the lilac jumpsuit, John, and not making a fool of herself that she'd not seen the young man come in. But come in he had, when the kusa grass was first set alight, though he did not endeavor to make his presence known. After apologizing profusely to the sexy yet unassuming intern and paying the suggested ten-dollar donation, he'd discreetly assumed a cushion in a corner at the back and just watched. A John Lennon-type, he was dressed all in black with his hair pulled into a small straw-colored bun. Although he was barely thirty, he aspired to be perceived as an old soul. When his turn to bow came, the youngish newcomer peered around the Zendo through his trendy samsara-shaped spectacles until his eyes landed on Dawn and lingered there, on her blond and black-robed form.

The skinny man in his skinny jeans wasn't afraid. Not of the middle-aged White lady joining the Japanese cult. Not of the intimidatingly beautiful intern, the tyrannical cushion mistress, the ambiguous priests, or the foreign deity. More than anything, he was curious and straightforward, a vessel emptied of questions looking to get filled up again.

The young newcomer strolled up to Dawn, peered curiously into her eyes, and smirked. When he chanted, he did so like a little boy trying out a tongue twister behind the swing set for the first time. His intonation went up at the end of each phrase like a question.

"Buddha recognizes Buddha? Buddha bows to Buddha?"

Afterward, they all enjoyed the prosecco and pecorino, which the pretty intern had so painstakingly put out. It tasted of the earth, of Europe. With great delight, Dawn mingled for photos, wept in the arms of friends, and thanked strangers like she loved them all. Even John, chatting too closely with the lilac intern, his knitted eyebrows signaling his intense interest and focus, could not stir up any animosity in her. She had admitted her sins before the entire sangha. They all knew who she really was, and she was still here with people smiling at her, which meant she was forgiven—forgiven for all except that which had transpired in the twenty-odd minutes (and counting) since the official forgiving. For that, Dawn knew she would have to die, be reborn, and ask for forgiveness all over again.

In the taxi home, Dawn was annoyed that John's cheeks were still ruddy from crying. She would have addressed it if she'd seen him wailing like that yesterday—taken him into the living room and pinned him there, in her favorite chair, till he had turned his consciousness inside out. The dissection of feelings would have driven him out into the streets and possibly the arms of a Chinatown masseur to recover, which would have hurt her. But his tears tonight needed no autopsy. Dawn knew why her husband had wept.

When they got to Grand Central Station, she said something vaguely about taking a trip upstate in the coming weeks, maybe to the Garrison Institute or the Shambhala retreat center in the Shawangunks. He was staring out the window at the one sex shop left on Sixth Avenue. *Does he hear me?* She would never know. He sighed as if the idea of being Buddhist together now that she was officially Buddhist was taking all the fun out of Buddhism.

"So, dear," he finally managed, "what did they put on the back of your rakusu?"

"I don't know. I haven't looked."

"That's ridiculous. Can I see?"

"No, you can't."

After the divorce, Dawn stopped attending dokusan with Sensei Kyodo.

"Grief is merely the lion roaring," he told her when she told him she was considering stepping back from all religion/spiritual practice until the divorce was finalized. "Let us help you heal."

Eleven months later, she went in to resign from the sangha and discovered that the hateful intern was a rather well-adjusted doctoral student in neuropsychology who went by her dharma name, Dai-En. She was already carrying John's second first child.

Though she went back to eating red meat and never set foot in the Zendo again, Dawn continued to pay the Zen center's monthly dues out of a kind of lazy guilt (or the tax write-off). Tithing made her feel better, just as it had made her parents feel better when they cut checks to the Episcopal Church, whose sanctuary they only entered on Christmas Eve and Easter Sunday. These Manhattan monks were not aging Anglicans questioning their relevance in a world that increasingly belonged to the religious nones. They were twenty-first-century incarnations of Avalokiteshvara—they accepted her checks. Eventually, they stopped calling to make sure she was alright. They were compassionate professionals. They understood.

The rakusu went to the "museum." Namely, it was folded and placed into Dawn's wide-mouthed Muji box, where she stashed essential randomness. You know, spiritual things.

The seasons turned. Manhattan stayed the same, though all its residents swore the city was experiencing unprecedented real estate chaos and political upheaval. She stopped riding in taxis and stuck to walking or riding the subway. Once, at Astor Place, she encountered an Asian-looking artist with a broken thumb who sold beautiful calligraphy that reminded her of the Zendo in a safely abstract way. She'd approached him to buy one, but he'd turned her away, sending her off with a handmade card stamped with his thumbprint in red.

"Find me again," he'd said, "and maybe I'll sell you something."

She looked for him for a while whenever descending into the city's subterranean belly, but the artist was just another of its hungry ghosts, soon forgotten. Eventually, she let go of the idea that possessing one of his works to hang in her new, post-divorce apartment might serve as the perfect symbol of her Zen exploits. Instead, she relinquished all notion of symbols, experimented with Sufism, went paleo, wore all black during the day, and lay at night in a loft in Bed-Stuy beside the young John Lennon, who had no dharma name, only a regular name, Sean.

The day of Dawn's jukai had been Sean's first and only visit to the Zendo. One of his AA buddies had recommended meditation, and his therapist had concurred. It didn't help, but Dawn did. She loved him and paid his bills until he could find work, an act like throwing a rope ladder into the hole of his despair. After a month of dating, she bought him a dozen polypropylene boxes from Muji and neatly tidied away all his possessions inside of them. He wrote songs that no one heard except Dawn. She introduced him to her daughter, who was just a few years younger than he was. And when he didn't want to fuck Maya more than he wanted to fuck her, she loved him even more.

Sean gifted Dawn a pair of trendy, samsara-shaped spectacles for their first Christmas together, just like his. He'd bought them for her even though she did not need prescription glasses. He just thought they might amuse her, and that was reason enough. At least since he had known her, Dawn's vision had always been pretty good.

Stand Clear of the Closing Doors, Please

THEY SHARED sufficiently similar geography regarding their ancestry to appease old-fashioned Korean grandparents, though their childhood socioeconomics couldn't have been more different. Both grew up passing, though Sam, adopted by an oncologist and his interior decorator wife, was never aware that "failing" was ever an option. She grew up not feeling any different until that was all she was. And, by then, it was too late.

The couple was always surprised whenever the question imposed itself without fail: *No, but where are you* from? The answers never changed.

He was from a tiny town in rural Oregon. And she was from Greenwich, Connecticut.

The latte with long foam chosen over the quick filter drip, a last-minute outfit change, an Uber arriving in the wrong place, a zealous humanities professor incapable of curtailing his content—all of it made them both uncharacteristically late for their first date. But it was the lateness that made them arrive at the meeting point at the same time, making the moment feel something like fate.

Though Sam often bragged that she was "physically incapable" of being sexually attracted to another Asian, recognition sparked on the steps of the Low Memorial Library beneath the unchanging bronze gaze of Alma Mater. Charlie suggested they meet there "to see if they liked each other's faces in real life, al fresco," before committing to a coffee, cocktail, or the like.

Like the *Mona Lisa*, the statue's resting face perpetuated enigma. She was either suppressing a smile, loathe to bestow her lofty praise for fear of encouraging mediocrity, or entrenched in an intractable state of perpetual disapproval.

They looked like they belonged together, but not in the sibling way. Both were skinny, with black glasses, dressed in stripes, and crowned with glossy black hair and almost-straight teeth.

Winter came back suddenly, just before the weekend. The snow that fell was unwelcome because it was the kind of late-season snow that is useless for skiing because all the resorts, except for Mammoth, thousands of miles away in California, have just closed. Aggressive redoubling of frost undermined the daffodils and tulips attempting to bud from Washington Square Park to pots on Park Avenue patios. Optimists, who'd migrated to Manhattan from warmer states and prematurely stashed their winter layers away, collapsed into a hyperbolic and immobilized state. But on Wall Street, spring snow did not matter. Only Friday did.

The Dow closed up 99.13 points. Charlie's work buddies started with the cocaine around lunch. Every week it was the same. They invited him to join the "shit-fuck-fest." He wasn't afraid of getting caught or addicted. He was an Asian American man who excelled at math, played no instruments, and was a decent sea kayaker. He'd gone to Columbia on a scholarship, need based. Charlie believed his banker buddies had perfected performative affirmative action; they didn't want him around any more than he wanted to pretend to be some bro that he was not. An extroverted introvert, long days at the office zapped all his energy for social interactions. When the markets closed, so did he. His capacity for existence dwindled to little more than his weed pen and minimal interactions with food delivery people. None of his colleagues were married yet, so he always used his wife as an excuse.

"You know I'd love to, but Sam's got theater tickets."

"You know I'd be there in a heartbeat, but Sam's got dinner reservations."

"You know I would, dudes, but Sam's pregnant." (She was not, but it was true that they were sort of trying.)

The conjugal reminder mitigated uncoolness on his terms. Not giving a fuck about specifics while still projecting an aura of success, no matter the cost, isn't that what adulting was increasingly all about?

The Fulton Street Subway stairs were slick with a wetness that couldn't decide if it wanted to freeze. They called for extra care. Charlie, like all the other commuters, was mesmerized by his phone. A barrage of controversial Supreme Court decisions had been detonating all day, and Charlie was just getting caught up when, suddenly, his brogue went out from under him on the penultimate step.

He grabbed the railing just in time to keep his legs from deserting him, crashing his body to the filthy floor. He rolled his torso instinctively upward, using a hip snap and forearm braced against the railing at ninety degrees. The other passengers were oblivious. Someone could fling themselves onto the tracks right in front of them, and they'd never notice till their phones pinged with the news alert. Only an old homeless Chinese guy selling framed calligraphy and six

Korean Christian fundamentalists had seen him almost fall. The artist said nothing while the evangelists asked in Korean if he was OK. When he pretended not to understand, they solicited some money.

A whoosh of humid, chilly subway air affronted. Then, the train charged into the station. Charlie stepped back while the rest of the incoming weekend crowd streamed by him, ramming on and off the train. He was standing too close to the platform edge in his attempt to get away from the Bible-wielding Koreans. He thought, briefly, of Asian stereotypes about suicide.

"Stand clear of the closing doors, please!"

Friday night, Sam was dressed in a pair of Charlie's boxer shorts from college and a Women's March sweatshirt. He remembered when tight dresses dominated her weekend sartorial lexicon, now banished. Not yet thirty, but she claimed years of wearing heels at prep school had deformed her pinky toes, just as the years of academic then career pressure and national politics had "deformed her soul." It had been about six months since she'd quit her job in publishing without any idea of what to do next. She'd been raised with every privilege a White person could dream of, yet she railed against capitalism, sexism, and disenfranchisement. Charlie, who'd grown up on tinned fish and clipped coupons, thought disenfranchisement was a lie the so-called "oppressed" told to justify their laziness.

Sam had recently entered her unwashed-hair era, part of her latest campaign against the chemical evils of corporate shampoo. It was still long and silky, though, and he loved it when she piled it up at the back of her skull and captured the black mass with a hot pink plastic claw. The haphazardness of the elegance rich girls possess (but poor girls do not) formed a significant part of Charlie's attraction to his wife. She was like a White girl in her cultural ownership but was not White—the best of both worlds. Hunched over their tiny, round kitchen table wielding magic markers, glitter, and a hot glue gun over a giant foam board, imagining her seven months pregnant or at the table doing arts and crafts with their young son or daughter was easy. But their son or daughter, the next generation, was still only a ghost of an idea. He peered over at his wife's latest project and groaned.

"STOP WHITE TERRORISM. THIS IS MY COUNTRY TOO, YOU FASCISTS," he read aloud. "Babe, do you really think rainbow glitter and fascism go well together?"

"Hey," she replied, ignoring the slight. She allowed her cranium to be kissed but otherwise barely batted an eye. "Did you take off your shoes?"

He had not but was about to. "Yep, sorry!"

Since George Floyd's murder and the blaming of Chinese people for the coronavirus, Sam had become "activated" (as she liked to say—the word *woke* made her cringe). Her libido, however, seemed to have vanished with the dawning of her political conscience. Hillary Clinton lost; then, suddenly, all the creative vigor and passion Sam used to put into pleasing her husband now went into her politics. The first anniversary of the Atlanta spa shootings was coming up, sending Sam and her newish organizer friends into hyperdrive. The girls were planning to attend a rally for the movement against anti-Asian violence that Saturday in Union Square. Charlie was against her going because it seemed unsafe. While she used to like it when he ordered for her at restaurants, now, she swiftly shut down at the first sign of anything he did that resembled uxorial control.

"That's ridiculous, Charlie. Your mind is backward. This is New York. The subway is the safest place on earth. There aren't racist lumberjacks running around with chainsaws here."

When would Sam's zeal for solidarity and community fade like her house music phase? Charlie's mother wanted to know why they weren't having a baby now that Sam had quit her job. Charlie's childhood best friend, Jim, who now lived in DC, was the only one who knew how long it had been since Charlie had last fucked his wife. They'd only talked about it once, during Jim's last visit. They'd pounded Old Fashions in midtown when Jim's train had been delayed due to weather. Two brothers, wasted with tomato-red faces.

"Chicks aren't like us, brother. They don't get turned on by multiple things at once," Jim had tried to console.

But Jim had gone to college on a snowboarding scholarship with a revolving door of girlfriends who never stuck around much longer than the snow. He did not understand where Charlie was coming from.

"Don't worry, dude. This woke shit'll pass. My girl's suddenly all into it too. But then a new season of *Real Housewives* is gonna start, and that'll be that. Like, we Asians aren't oppressed. Not like Black people, anyway. Let her march and knit pussy hats or whatever. Just ignore it, don't feed into the energy, and she'll be back. It's just a phase."

If it was only a phase, it was now threatening to stretch into a second presidential term. Sure, the world could be considered a terrifying place for women who looked like Sam, but Charlie knew everything would be alright. Upward trends boded well for all. Bull gives way to bear, then back to bull again, just like in nature. All that marriage asked of him was that he be patient and pretend to be supportive. That was the "for better or for worse" part. Jim would be a bachelor forever, so it didn't matter if he didn't understand.

Charlie pulled on his weed pen while Sam continued to work on her protest posters with headphones on. She was listening to a podcast based on a book one of her friends, who was really into the AAPI stuff, had given her: *Chasing the Tiger's Tail: Radical Forgiveness* by Sally Oh. She wanted her husband to read it, but he did not want to read anything besides Thomas Piketty and *The Wall Street Journal.* The weed strain was a new hybrid he'd never tried before. It tasted earthy and mellowed him out.

"Want some?"

She didn't.

"What? You're too high on life now or something? What happened to fun, Sam?"

He put on a stand-up special she'd been talking about all week on Netflix, but apparently, she'd already watched it without him. They ordered Thai food and slurped curry out of separate containers without speaking. They used to order three dishes to share and then scoop them out of their plastic containers into three beautiful ceramic bowls they'd purchased from a cute Japanese shop on East 9th Street when they'd first moved in together. But lately, each procured their respective favorites, kept their noodles cordoned, and that was that.

They curled up on opposite ends of the sectional without touching. Sam's phone mesmerized her with its infinite scroll of op-eds and breaking news, followed by more op-eds. Charlie faded in and out of sleep. He only ambled off to bed when the late-night shows came on. Their bedroom was a glorified walk-in closet with a full-sized bed, which Sam kept wistfully saying wasn't big enough.

"What we really need is a California king."

"That doesn't sound very feminist. Maybe we need a California monarch to be gender-neutral."

"You're such a dick. You know that, right?"

Sam stayed up until one o'clock, finishing three posters in all—just in case someone showed up at the rally without. So far as her husband knew, she was completely sober. By the time she made her way into their bedroom in full-length, button-up pajamas, he was about to begin masturbating for the second time that night. His hand was on his shaft when his wife's warm body sliced into the sheets beside him. He reached for her, hopefully.

"Not tonight, babe."

Sam pushed Charlie away, then curled up on her opposing hip facing the window with the fire escape.

"Goodnight, babe."

Charlie woke up alone. Even on weekdays, that was normal. Since Sam quit her job, she went for a run every morning before the sun rose.

"It's my favorite part of living in the city," she'd explained when he'd first pushed back on this suspicious new ritual, citing qualms about her safety. "I love the streets when the light's all black-blue, and no one can see me. It's like I'm a ghost. All the barriers and loneliness evaporate."

He assumed that's where she went and failed to notice that the glittery posters were gone. Since it was Saturday, he hoped she'd return with bagels, lox, and fresh coffee. She did not. He texted her, but she did not reply. He fetched himself a bowl of cereal, pulled on his weed pen, and returned to bed. There he stayed, watching MMA on his tablet. Around noon, he got up, showered, and called his mother. They discussed his work, eating habits, laundry, and plans to have a baby very soon, please.

And where is Sam today? His mother wanted to know. *I want to say hello to Sam.*

"I told you, Ma, she's with her girlfriends. Yes, Ma, that's right, she's really into 'community stuff' right now. But don't worry. She'll be home this afternoon. We're planning to go to the Container Store and do groceries."

Sam didn't come home after the rally ended. The Container Store was having a sale, but Charlie thought it would be pathetic to go alone. He texted her again, annoyed that she'd gone off to a post-protest brunch with her girlfriends and had plans "downtown" for the rest of the day. He became pissed but did not articulate how he was feeling to anybody.

Charlie's pattern, you see, expressed itself very passive-aggressively. He'd inherited this mode of being from his father, who'd learned it from his father, who'd been the first to migrate and settle in the West. Even though Charlie wanted to shout at his wife and possibly even shake her delicate shoulders, he put on a baseball cap, took off his watch, and went crosstown to do what he wanted. *Let her neglect me to save the world. I'm not going to ignore myself in the meantime.*

Like most uptown dwellers, Charlie detested going downtown on weekends. The subway was the culprit— weekend trains crammed with tipsy B&Ts. You couldn't pay him to grace the Union Square farmers market or see any plays off-Broadway. When he was not working, he liked to walk, especially through Central Park, stopping now and then to occupy a green bench, pull on his pen, and people-watch.

Despite the chill, he decided to stroll to clear his head. The park wasn't deserted. People were rebelling against the prolonging of winter. Strolling and drinking coffees, their dogs tangled leashes as they tried to sniff each other. He walked off some of his resentment and decided to reroute toward the Whisked Bakery on the Upper West Side. Their lavender flan was Sam's favorite and, apparently, an aphrodisiac. Every time he brought her one, they fucked like they used to back in the dorms. The last time he indulged her, she even went down on him.

It was March 8, International Women's Day, which Charlie hadn't realized. Women weaving around outside the 72nd Street station handed out mimosas to other women passing by. Even though the flower-giving tradition had been started more than half a century ago by Italian feminists, he thought it was a new thing started by AAPI to help "Stop Asian Hate." They reminded Charlie of the first bouquet he'd ever presented to Sam. On their first anniversary, Charlie hadn't had any money to buy fancy flowers, so he'd stolen a dozen daisies from one of the beds lining the quad.

A twenty-something blond in leggings and a metallic puffy jacket caught his eye and smiled at him. Suddenly, all Charlie wanted was one of the bright yellow sprigs with the wavy, spread-out blossoms. The flowers looked so energetic and lively in the pretty blond girl's hand. She was holding them like she wanted to share them with someone special. Wasn't he special?

He approached her and asked, "Can I have a flower, please?"

The leggings took one step back. Blue eyes gaped at him with pity and confusion.

"Um, no. We're handing these out in honor of International Women's Day as a sign of mutual respect and support. They're for women only. Sorry."

The lavender flan and a bouquet of bodega daisies lay beside a candle lit hopefully around when Charlie expected Sam to return. But she did not return. Brunch must have metamorphosed into shopping, drinks, and possibly dinner.

Alone in his sanctuary of sweatpants, he pulled on his pen and drifted off to sleep without even bothering to masturbate.

The tinkling of a metal fork on a porcelain plate woke him. It was still night, the deadest part, which coincides with the taxi shift change, the closing of pizza shops, and the opening of bakeries.

"Babe?"

There was no answer. Charlie shuffled out into the kitchen with no idea what time it was. His wife, finally, was home, still dressed in her pink pussy hat and running clothes. He could not tell if she'd just come back from being out all night or was about to head out for her predawn run. She licked the last of the flan from a fork. Her neck looked unusually long. Her hair was down and … blow-dried? Its glossy sheen was illumined blue and orange from the lights streaming in from the street. He approached her sleepily, reaching for her waist, but she stepped back.

"Everything alright, babe? Where've you been?"

No answer. Instead, she just pointed to the yellow flowers as she devoured the last of the flan then and grinned.

"These," she said finally. "They're really beautiful. I guess you do love me after all."

Charlie woke up alone, which surprised him, as it had been very late when they had gone back to bed. Their lovemaking had been as it once was. Not too soft or hard, with her sometimes on top, lasting about twenty minutes. He recalled with a grin how their passion had even been so loud it had summoned a disgruntled neighbor to the door. Intense as a SWAT team, the pounding had only lasted a few minutes before the poor lonely soul had given up and returned to his empty apartment to seethe alone at the passion of others. They'd fallen asleep with their noses brushing, his palm on her hips and lower abdomen. Their bodies had been so synchronized he was convinced a baby might have taken hold.

"Babe?"

No answer. Yellow light streamed into the apartment sideways, which was empty. The red numbers on the kitchen stove told him it was almost eleven. How did it get so late? How much had he smoked? The plate with the flan rested in the sink, still traced with frosted crumbs. The daisies had been moved on the windowsill, the petal edges starting to wilt just the tiniest bit in the direct sun. The fancy candle had burned itself out. *Shit. There's forty bucks*

49

gone. His phone was cradled on the couch, completely dead. Annoyed, he scooped it up and plugged it in.

Just then, the buzzer screamed. Whoever it was pressed repeatedly. The long shrill sound bored into Charlie's half-dazed ear. He loafed over to the intercom.

"What the fuck? Who is this?"

"Charlie, it's me, man. Thank fucking god. Buzz me up."

"Jim? The fuck are you doing here?"

Jim was at the top of the stairs three minutes later, hugging a bewildered Charlie, who was still in his boxers. There were tears in his eyes.

"I'm so sorry, man. I took the first train up after I saw the news late last night and couldn't reach you. You scared the shit out of me. It's just so fucking fucked up. This whole country. Shit. I can't believe it."

"Saw what?"

Charlie's phone gasped back to life. Everyone he knew except his mother had texted him, and his voice mailbox was full of known and unknown numbers.

"Oh fuck me. You don't know yet, do you? Haven't the cops called you? What the actual fuck …"

Jim said some more words, but Charlie no longer comprehended. The news alert was suddenly his whole world. His own personal hell world, adorned with yellow flowers.

"Young Asian woman first believed to be a suicide was pushed to her death at a subway station in Union Square late Saturday afternoon in what city officials are calling an 'unprovoked' attack."

The Scott Plot[1]

THE LAST TIME THE SCOTT FAMILY visited Jane's Oma, she did not know their faces. Jane's father shouted for the whole hour, mainly at the Black and Brown khaki-clad women in charge of dressing and feeding the elderly White Americans like zoo animals. Little Jane, meanwhile, perched at the end of the mechanical bed beside her German grandmother, smoothing the dry, hay-colored wisps from her furrowed forehead.

Just a few years ago, things had been the reverse: Jane's mother and father would go gallivanting at restaurants or the theater while Oma hurried across

[1] This story was first published in the summer 2019 issue of Delay Fiction as "Burying the Hatchling."

the Oma Bridge from Jersey to cook Jane's favorite spaghetti with vegetables, then bathe her body and brush her hair. At first, Oma's brushing was painful. This violent untangling was not deliberate, like when Jane's mother did it ("indifference to pain is beauty"), but rather a lack of familiarity. Her technique softened as Oma's understanding of foreign follicles increased with time.

Jane reciprocated the care now that life was gliding by her grandma in a marzipan glaze in which salons played no part. She implemented the same brushing technique her grandmother eventually developed to work through the stubborn gnarls without causing excessive, undue pain. She clenched a fistful of her grandmother's hair, just three inches below the roots. The dye on the lightweight locks had faded to a color resembling sugar cookies. They were so thin she raked her fingers through them like air. Jane braced the comb against the curl of her grandmother's skull to not painfully tear a single follicle from its root. Oma did not speak while Jane worked. She was too busy being suspicious, eyeballing all the non-White staff. Occasionally, she'd squirm and gape at Jane with that same suspicious look and start. Wide open and punctuated with cloudy, cornflower irises, her grandmother's eyes bored into her like she was the enemy.

Alzheimer's.

When the doctor in Jersey first told the family, on the ride home, because the passenger seat was bereft of her mother, Jane felt safe enough to remark to her father, "At least it sounds German."

On the morning of Oma's funeral, Jane straps into the black patent leather Mary-Janes that her mother bought her for "churchy occasions." Still, the heat and humidity have expanded her feet without her permission. The shoes pinch. Jane knows "pinching" (or pain in general) is not an excuse but avoids putting them on anyway, these coffins for children's feet, and makes figure eights on the carpet in white ruffle socks. Her mother, meanwhile, preens about the Yellow Room. The spare bedroom never hosts guests because it has served as Jane's mother's glorified boudoir ever since Jane's grandmama, the matriarch back in Taiwan, suffered a stroke and almost died. Her mother keeps all her Asian things in that room and locks the door when she's away. As Jane's father frowns and says, "Too much Oriental clutter clashes with the rest of our decor. It makes our taste appear too 'eclectic' and 'themed.'"

The only time he goes in there and says these things are when they have someplace to be, but Jane's mother is not yet dressed. For Jane's mother, her mother-in-law's funeral is not an occasion for mourning. Celebration, perhaps, or just an ordinary day where she is expected to put her exotic self on display for her husband and his people—and deliver.

Jane enters the adult realm presided over by her mother to find her balanced on a Turkish ottoman before the black lacquer vanity in a silk robe, parsing through some of Oma's jewelry. She wants to honor Oma by wearing a brooch or necklace that once belonged to her when they put her in the hole in the ground. But it's already been more than an hour of accessorizing before the vanity, and Jane knows the truth because her mother never tried to hide it from her. Her mother always detested her mother-in-law because, as Jane's mother loves to say, "Your Oma is a *lacist* Nazi."

Jane's mother, then, is not honoring so much as appraising. Jane drifts away from her mother only to encounter her father marauding anxiously in the hall with a sweaty glass of Sancerre.

"Go check on your mother." But what he really means is: *How fucking late are we going to be to my mother's funeral?*

There's no point in "talking back," so Jane nods. She turns and again crosses the threshold of her golden maternal kingdom. In the boudoir-turned bunker, all the walls are painted sunflower yellow. The girl knows from experience how the erratic movements of a child moving through her mother's space create great rage in her, so she tries to creep in with the dignity usually reserved for adolescents demanding to be taken seriously. She is fascinated by that koi-colored room full of things that belong to her but also do not, and soon she forgets to focus on keeping her poise.

Her eyes drift around. Fingers follow. The girl feels contaminated by her father's restlessness and is thus compelled to communicate that to her mother using her child's body. She creeps around like a shadow on a partly cloudy, windy day. Again, her mother ignores her. Instead of "doting American mom," she performs East Asian woman in the West: frigid, fragile, and feminine. Namely, all the things Jane's mother never tires of reminding Jane she's too coarse and Caucasian ever to be.

Jane wants her mother's acknowledgment but knows what is asked for is rarely given. She does what her father does when he wants attention without asking directly: She clears her throat and *ahems*. The mother's middle back quivers, but she does not turn to speak to her child.

One tanned crane leg protrudes. It is smooth and shaped like a kayak paddle as she braces it against the carpet. Then, with four slim fingers, she unrolls another of the midnight velvet pouches. Oma's pearls emerge. Over her mother's shoulder and into the mirror, Jane ogles the strand of little white moons in her ocher hands. Jane tries not to let her mother see her daughter seeing her, even though she knows her mother knows she does and probably wants an audience.

"Come here, girl." Though her mother barks into the mirror without turning around, Jane jumps and does as commanded. Jane's mother squeezes her jaw so that her tongue falls open, then shoves the pearls inside. "What do you think? Are they freshwater or fished out of the sea? Tell me, girl, have you inherited your mother's ability to *taste* value?"

They taste of salt, not grit. Jane reports as much to her mother, which causes her to sigh with disgust before snatching the necklace away. The mother rolls one, two, then three pearls into her lychee beak. In Mandarin, she whispers something to the mirror. It sounds like "delicious."

Footsteps in the corridor. Jane's father stomps abruptly into the Yellow Room. He shouts at Jane's mother like he shouted at the khaki women who fed and washed Oma at the home: "Just get on with it, Wing! No one is coming to the funeral. No one. All my relatives are dead. All my mother's friends are dead. The dead don't care how you dress."

At first, Jane's mother pretends she is alarmed. Her husband *never* comes into the Yellow Room, and that's how she likes it. But then, she composes herself with a snort. When she does that, she looks like a dragon. Not a lady born in the Year of the Dragon, but a real one.

"That's obscene American stuff. In *my* country, what you wear to a funeral is how you pay respect." Jane's mother levitates from the Turkish ottoman, scoops up the *International Herald Tribune,* and starts thumbing through the sports section. "Sports are vulgar in every country."

Jane's father snatches the newspaper and tears it in two. She ignores him and turns on CNN, the international edition. There is something on about fixing market rates and China. The ticker at the bottom informs that Anderson Cooper, Jane's mother's favorite, will be on momentarily. Though he is in a war zone, Anderson looks handsome in his unwrinkled safari shirt. An "ooh" escapes Jane's mother's lips as she plops down on the French daybed smothered in batik textiles to watch.

"Wing, I know what you're doing! Today is not the day to be a bitch. Get dressed. I'm burying my fucking mother. Where is your goddamned sense of decency? Do you hear me, Wing? I'm going to the funeral home right now. And I'm taking the child. Meet us there, and *don't* be late."

Jane's mother grins and turns up the volume so that Anderson Cooper, who never shouts, is now yelling. Jane's father storms out of the Yellow Room, his bleary blue eyes bolted ahead like a bird's. He forgets that he is supposed to take his daughter with him. She's been waiting to trail after him away from her mother this whole time, like a duckling, but the door has already slammed.

Jane's mother mutes the television. She smiles tightly and expels breath through her nostrils, which flare like bluebell flowers on a breezy day. "He's just acting shamefully because he misses his mommy. So, girl, are you staying with your mother or going off with *him*?"

Jane does not know how to respond without further angering one parent or the other, so she remains mute. If it goes on too long, her silence will mutate into "disrespect" and infuriate her mother, who will then *make* her daughter respond. Thankfully, an elevator ding breaks the silence, stretched with tension, and Jane's father is gone.

It will be seven minutes before the elevator can journey down to the lobby and then come back up again. Seven minutes with a dragon is an eternity. Jane throws her mother a condescending look of disdain, which she has learned from her father, buckles up her coffin shoes, then totters through winces after him, down twelve flights of concrete stairs.

When Oma first flew away to the nursing home, a coop buried so deep into New Jersey it was almost Pennsylvania (not that it mattered—she no longer discerned the difference), Jane's father crossed the Oma Bridge, went to the Big House, and returned to the Scott's Upper West Side apartment bearing bubble-wrapped treasures. The afternoon he carted home Oma's jewelry, Jane's mother noticed her aversion to inheritance and screeched at her to come into the Yellow Room to help her sort the treasures into piles. As she extracted each item, she did so with the morbidly sacred precision of an ancient Egyptian embalmer exacting the scalpel. She palmed each pewter, silver, or gold organ one by one as she weighed their fates: *sell, keep, not sure.*

Jane kept her tongue coiled against her teeth until a gold sparrow brooch with tiny, freshwater pearl eyes reported for judgment—the one Oma used to pin to the woolen Austrian walking hat that tilted aloft her oatmeal curls every time she left the house.

"*Birdie*," Jane remembered Oma whispering to her while getting her ready for bed one night, "*was the first gift your Opa ever gave me when he came from America with his army to liberate Germany after the war. Because we were young and still alive and in love. One day, my darling girl, when I am gone, birdie will be yours.*"

Birdie was the first item Jane's mother dumped into the "sell" pile.

"It's ugly. Your White family has terrible taste, not like your wàipo in Taipei. She's immaculate—colonially regal, like me. Like you will be, maybe, if you get out of this scrappy wood-urchin phase your Nazi grandma encourages. Excuse me, *encouraged*. No, no, girl, don't cry. You know I *loathe* excessive displays of emotion in children! Trust me, when you're older and cultivate a bit of style, you won't want any of this old European junk. It represents the past. It doesn't think it does, but it does, and they are just in denial. You'll see, girl. My mother's things are much, much nicer. I'm doing you a favor."

Jane's father forgets to wait in the lobby—or anywhere else. He has already moved his tall Aryan limbs into the sunshine with a stride three times as long as Jane's. Jane loosens her kneecaps to catch him, but before she can traverse the block, the gap between them has grown too big for her sapling legs to close unless she runs. Her black velvet funeral dress will stick to her skin if she speeds up. Her mother will yell that because she's ruined her dress, she's also ruined her grandmother's funeral.

Jane resists breaking into a jog, but the fabric itches. Instead, she measures her paces but elongates their arc, attempting to hop from crack to crack between the sidewalk slabs. But each one is as long as her length, and there are too many cracks. Her feet start to balloon from the heat. Growing pockets of flesh push against the tight patent leather, blistering the sides of her heels and little toes. Still, she tracks her father's dark gray suit winding away from her as fast as her wàipo's wàipo, whose feet were bound.

Jane's mother likes to tell Jane this story about foot binding whenever she's irate about something she calls "your disobedience." Not as family history or cultural knowledge but as a threat of future punishment for mysterious, intergenerational crimes.

The funeral home is a large, non-offensive brownstone on the corner of 81st and Madison. A young man in a black suit stands outside the fancy death building guarding a Cadillac hearse blooming with fresh-cut flowers. Jane's mother is already there, proudly swanning out of a taxi. She must have tipped the driver handsomely to speed and overtake her husband on foot. She is fingering the carnelian juzu beads Wàigōng brought her back from the Asakusa Shrine when he took a business trip to Tokyo when Jane's mother was Jane's age. She poses on the corner looking like a 1920s actress in a silent film about a war-won jade bride. In the window of the cashmere boutique across the street, a sign proclaims *SALE*. The wind breathes up Jane's mother's skirt, and her eyes wide as wontons salivate over a periwinkle cardigan.

Her mother's ensemble is elegant but eggshell. She arrived dressed in a pleated crepe de chine skirt and matching jacket. Her husband greets her as appropriate for Madison Avenue, unconsciously and automatically reviewing her outfit. First, he experiences pleasure because he is a blond man from New Jersey married to a beautifully exotic creature. Anger is secondary. And for that, namely, her capacity to undermine just by being, he is incensed all the more.

"Jesus, Wing. What the fuck are you wearing white for?"

"In my country …"

"We're not in *your* country."

Jane's father snatches Jane's mother by the wrist and yanks her inside *just a little too hard.* The doorman turns away politely. His corporate overlords have trained him not to notice when clients misbehave. *Grief does crazy things to rich people.* Service people are thus told not to intervene in the drama until liability outweighs the dangers of the privileged feeling their feelings versus their perceptions of poor customer service.

Alzheimer's was invisible on Oma for many years. She came from hearty, Aryan stock—with a little Norwegian thrown in for bonus points. By the end, even she was no longer blond. First, she went hoary, then totally see-through. Cerulean veins streaked the backs of her alabaster palms. They looked to Jane like tiny jet streams in an inside-out sky when she stroked them one by one, imagining they were sky trails leading someplace wonderful. Even though, for four years, grown-ups told Jane that her grandmother could not understand or remember her, she always talked to her like she still knew.

She talked to her grandma about what was happening at school—her teachers, friends, and enemies. She went on at length about the cruelty of parents and homework before relishing their shared summertime rituals (which, Jane was sure, they'd perform again when Oma got better and escaped this lonely place). During her weekly visits to the place she secretly referred to as *The Old People Plantation*, Jane told her grandmother how she'd again cross the Oma Bridge over the Hudson to Paramus to stay with her on weekends at the Big House, where her father was once little. She promised they'd resurrect their little raised-bed plot, which they used to wake up with the sprinklers just before dawn and then clear raspberries from the heavy vines clinging to the garden walls for stirring into their breakfast yogurt.

On sun-drenched summer afternoons, they'd sometimes sit on rocks and spread out Jane's pink plastic tea party set on a willow stump. Oma would regale her with tales of the mountains in Austria, Opa, and the war. Whenever the history they were learning about in school awkwardly activated her grandmother's memories, Oma would smooth the hair on Jane's brow and sigh, "That was all a very long time ago, my dear Janey. And you know, the Second World War was tricky because both sides had a cause."

Everything inside the fancy funeral home is oxblood. The brocade walls, the gloomy chandelier, the Ottoman rugs, and the Chesterfield with clawed iron feet. On a marble credenza beneath a gilded mirror stands an ivory Saint Michael on one leg inside a glass box clutching a flaming sword. Jane wants to touch it and see if it vanishes—*poof*—but disapproving employee eyes warn her chubby fingers away.

A bald funeral director appears wearing a diagonal smile. He extends his hand in perfected reverent sorrow. Jane's father clamps it with sealed lips and makes an *mmm* sound.

"Mr. Scott, welcome. I am so sorry for your loss. Can I offer you some coffee? Tea? Champagne?"

"Champagne."

"Very good, ma'am. And for you, sir?"

"Bourbon will do."

"Right away, sir."

"Hey! Can I get a lemonade, please?"

Jane cries her order aloud too late. Moments later, the silver tray arrives devoid of any nonalcoholic beverages.

"Now, Mr. and Mrs. Scott," the bald funeral director explains, "everything is ready, just like you arranged. After the viewing, a limousine will take you to the cemetery, where the Lutheran minister from your mother's German parish will be waiting. The car will wait to return you to the city for lunch at Günter Seeder. Please, follow me. The visitation room is right this way."

Jane's father slugs, and her mother swishes, but Jane remains rooted as the Japanese knotweed that has been mercilessly attacking the rear of Oma's garden for as long as she can remember. A gaunt attendant wearing white gloves rakes back the old elevator grille.

Her mother steps inside the moveable coffin and twirls like a model at the end of the runway.

"Get in here, girl. Right now!"

Jane shakes her head *no*.

"Don't make me …" Her mother raises her voice, but the bald funeral director and his staff lower their eyes, so she softens her tone. "And why not, *darling girl?* Don't you want to see your precious Nazi grandmother one last time?"

"She wasn't actually a Nazi. And no, Not like that."

"She was, girl. She actually was!" Jane's mother cackles like one of the mean girls at school (with whom she pressures Janey to be friends). "And by *like that*, do you mean *dead?* Surely, you're too old to be scared of corpses? It's just a little biology in action, girl—nothing to be afraid of. You will be a corpse one day, not too long too. Hmmm."

"No. The dead don't scare me. I just don't want to see *her* like *that*."

Jane's mother snatches her wrist and yanks *just a little bit too hard*.

"Now, you listen to me, girl. In *my* country, we sit with the dead while they're dying until they're all the way dead. And when they're dead, we sit with them some more. Then we take the corpses to burn. We even chant things at the corpses and offer them tea and rice. We watch the corpses burn until the bones char, and then we go in after them with our priests and very long, very special chopsticks. Don't make that face, girl. Otherwise, it'll stay ugly like that forever. You'll be so sorry you used up what Asian beauty was in you in anger when you are left with a Western potato face. What was I saying? Ah, yes! Death! Death! It's perfectly natural. The only way to accept death is to *see* it. Otherwise, it isn't real, and you get sucked into a cycle of stupidity and sadness—that's all the Christian religion is."

The juzu beads jangle. Jane glances at her father. His begging bowl eyes are fixed on the wall between the crucifix and the clock while he gulps down her mother's half-sipped champagne.

"Daddy?"

Jane's father doesn't look at his daughter or wife. He studies the crucifix. His chest heaves as if heavy stones are crushing it.

"Wing, if she doesn't want to see her dead grandma's body, then she doesn't have to see her dead grandma's body. It's her first encounter with death—shock enough for a small child. Why are you always so creepy and morbid, anyway? Call me a racist again if you must, but I don't think it is cultural. It's just unnecessary, your bluntness. What kind of mother is so cold? No wonder the Taiwanese are the way they are, so isolated on the geopolitical stage. Today is hard enough. Let's just get on with it, shall we? I hate to keep the minister waiting. Germans are very punctual, as you know."

Dragon anger brims in Jane's mother's little crane-like body. Jane can feel it boiling and is afraid.

"Oh, yes, dear, everyone knows how *Germans* are. Fine. Have your way if you like. All day today, I'll allow it. It's *your* mother's funeral, after all."

Wing turns to her daughter. The dragon is still there, flying in playful circles inside her pupils. She takes on a conspiratorial tone, a favorite tactic when her attempts to bully or bribe her child into doing what she wants (usually against Jane's father) fail. "OK, girl, this is your last chance. Once they bury your Oma, she's gone. You can never say auf Wiedersehen again."

When she says auf Wiedersehen, the guttural indulgence of those spreading syllables at the back of her throat is too much, and she bursts out laughing. Jane's father scowls at her. The White people who work in the funeral home support the husband with sympathetic looks. But nobody is looking at Jane, even though she is the only child in this building of embalmed grown-up bodies, trembling a little and tearing up. "Bu—but I've never said goodbye forever to anyone before …"

Jane's father, by now, has had enough. *Children's brains and feelings are an intrusion that never stops.* He points to the Chesterfield beside the archangel without looking at Jane. Actually, he is looking at her forehead. "You wait there. Talk to that cross and ask God to take good care of Oma. Who knows, maybe it'll do you some good. Wing, come."

Up Jane's parents go. They trot solemnly behind the bald undertaker to see whether he has embalmed Oma so she looks dozy in her mahogany box lined with violet satin sleeping bags.

Jane can tell that her father is not thinking about God or Oma, only about himself and the Bordeaux he will swallow at lunch after the free whisky is finished. Bordeaux, then brandy, billed to Oma's estate as a tax write-off.

Something reeks of old ladies and science class. The young man dressed all in black, whom Jane first clocked when they arrived because, apart from her, he is the youngest and darkest-skinned person in the place, hovers nearby. He has been tasked with ensuring the kid doesn't smash Saint Michael or anything else valuable to smithereens while her parents view her grandmother's dead body. Since it's a funeral home and not a therapist's office, there are no incomplete puzzles or board games with missing pieces to pass a child's time appropriately.

The man in black whispers something to a colleague who passes by, staring at Jane. A moment later, the silver tray reappears. This time, it is carrying a glass filled with ice and lemonade. It's so cold that the glass is sweating. The liquid is the color of Oma's dandelion apron, the one she always used for baking in the summer.

"Thank you!" It feels icy in Jane's throat and tummy. "Yum."

The corners of the kind man's mouth turn up in the only smile allowed in that place. His smile says *this is no place for a kid.* Jane grins back. Where youth is shared, there is usually agreement.

Jane finishes her lemonade, then stands up and drifts past the archangel and crucifix toward the funeral home's front doors. The young man in black does not stop her. Outside, the sun blazes. It feels hot on her dark clothes. More than anything, she wants to kick off her coffin shoes, race into Central Park, and press her ribs against its tallest shale shelves—the ones they couldn't grind to asphalt when they created the park because the bedrock rising from her city's bones protects its heart.

Always, she feels better outside. Away from her parents and Oma's pickled remains, Jane forgets that she is supposed to behave and begins to speak as children do when they are not bored, anxious, or nervous. She speaks as freely as she would with one sneaker on the gravel while the other mounts the jungle gym, searching for a solid enough foothold before, at the encouragement of her friends, her entire body begins to climb. She paces the sidewalk as she chatters, sharing a random scientific fact about the rocks in the park. The man in black has siblings not much older than Jane, so he acts like he's never heard any of this before. "That's so cool!"

Jane is shocked that this adult is listening to her talk about things that interest children, so she talks more. She talks more to this strange man than she's spoken all day, maybe all week, maybe since Oma died, or even first got sick. She supplies more scientific randomness and beams when he receives it and is impressed with all her "did you knows …"

Soon, she is no longer talking about rocks. Only Oma.

"My Oma and I used to …"

Jane tells this strange man about how her grandmother used to drive across the Oma Bridge in her mushroom-colored Saturn to look after her during those long weekends when Nanny went to Newark to cook and clean for her children. She tells him how, though Oma loved to scout the best rocks and point out the easiest footholds, she never climbed them herself, saying, "The limitless sky is for children to explore." Instead, she tells him, Oma used to wait with her feet on the ground to make sure it was safe for her granddaughter to come back down.

By the time Jane is relaying how Oma was the only grown-up she'd ever seen squat cross-legged in the dirt like a kid, she is bawling harder than she has since she fell off her bike in Riverside Park and shaved the skin off both her kneecaps. Through hiccupping tears, she confesses to the man in black about how much she will miss lying in the grass with Oma and smelling that lemony scent of fresh-mowed lawn alchemizing with thick floral perfume. She describes their beloved raised-bed garden, where grandmother and granddaughter used to grow the sweetest, tangiest raspberries. About how Oma always brought her a freshly picked batch when she visited the city. And how, whenever Jane ascended the enormous shale slabs in Central Park, Oma would open her picnic basket and take out raspberries for when Jane would eventually slide back down. Sometimes, she'd get so scared her granddaughter would fall that she'd tighten her fists so much that she'd crush the berries to jam.

"If Oma ever felt bad about squashing our snack, I'd just hug her and say, 'It's OK, Oma. They taste sweeter this way …'"

The sun moves while Jane talks and talks. Miraculously, the man in black listens the whole time. His eyes meet the child's while he nods and sighs occasionally. His lower lip wavers when she relays the part about the raspberries becoming jam, but no tears fall. Most importantly, he says nothing.

Not, "Don't worry, your grandma is in heaven with God."

Not, "I remember when *my* grandma died …"

Not, "Try to look on the bright side of things. The sun is still shining, isn't it?"

When Jane finishes, her words hang around like Oma's perfume. It makes her want to cry again, so she falls silent and gazes at her feet. That's when she notices the bloody little bundle. A tiny brown and feathered body lies eviscerated beside her coffin shoes. *Is it a baby bird? What's that called again? A hatchling? Is that right? Is it dead? Yes, yes. It is dead-dead.*

After plummeting from the nest, the tiny chick appears to have been crushed from life. Its viscera are reversed: Internal organs and exoskeleton are inside out. Intestines the color of crushed raspberries smear the sidewalk and shine like a scoop of raspberry sorbet dropped from a pricey Amorino cone. With the sun shining through them, her organs glow neon orange. The dead baby bird no longer has any wings, only their suggestion. Whatever was her body is now only an outline of soft, unfeathered plumage and gray toothpick bones.

Jane peers down at the tiny corpse over the coffin shoes. She is the first dead thing Jane has ever seen.

A dog comes along on a blue leash and lunges. Just before its jaws seize the little prize, the dog is heeled with a resolute yank. Jane throws herself onto the sidewalk, rubbing her knees into the cement, and entombs the dead bird in a dome made of her fingers. "No!"

The dog walker tosses the kid a confused glance before pretending that it did not just happen and loping wordlessly away. Jane takes no notice of the dog or its walker. She is glaring accusingly at the young man in black. "Don't just stand there looking at me! You're a funeral director. Let's direct her funeral."

"But I'm not—"

Tears roll. The man in black is close enough to his childhood that he knows Jane's tears won't stop until she gets what she wants or is punished for wanting it until all wanting gets canceled, and all desire buries itself away until midlife. Jane remains kneeling in the street, trembling in her lovely funeral dress. The sun hits her coffin shoes, making them shine. *Do I have to start bawling again?* But she doesn't. She doesn't even have to glance toward Central Park. The man in black already knows. He glances furtively left and then right as he breaks one million grown-up rules and takes Jane's hand.

"OK, kid. But we gotta be quick, alright? Or I'll lose more than just my job. Got it?"

The pair hurry down 81st Street, past the tourists swirling on the steps of the Metropolitan Museum, and break into a jog until the reservoir, where runners bounce up and down in a circle. Emerald treetops wave beyond the low stone wall that divides the city from the park. One redhead in his thirties, wearing an NYU Stern T-shirt, runs like the entire park is his private country estate. He runs without stopping for pedestrians or automobiles at designated crossings. He runs with his music turned up so he cannot hear anyone coming. He runs as if it's all his and nobody else's. As he cruises by, he checks the man in black with his shoulder, then huffs, "Watch it, man!" through pulsating headphones.

The man in black mumbles something about how runners are the worst then grabs Jane's hand and points to the pond.

"We gotta hurry. How about a burial at sea?"

In the other direction, birds chirp up a symphony. Jane glances that way, and her intended destination is understood. The wooded, winding network of paths at the park's heart, known as the

Ramble and styled after the Catskill Mountains, are so green and overgrown that it almost feels like Bear Mountain, where Oma used to take Jane in September to see the leaves turn. Bloated roots of a centuries-old pine mark a secret way in. Migrating birds repose in its branches because people who care for living things have strung up pine cones stickered with seed. Swallows chatter and nibble all around. They remind Jane of Oma's guests at her once-famed Christmas soirees.

Just beyond them, a primordial rock rises, and the girl runs toward its summit. The man in black does not follow. He stays on the ground below, holding the perimeter, his giant feet firmly planted. "I'll wait for you here in case you slip. For the love of God, kid, be careful!"

Jane's coffin shoes slide around on the slippery shale, so she tears them off, and her white ruffle socks, too. Bare feet smack stone, eagerly planting rough and cool kisses on her soles. Oma used to do that. Plant kisses, carrots, strawberries, and hang houses stocked with food for the birds. For the first time since Oma died, Jane smiles. The wind cruises through her hair, the air in her lungs is heating up, and her brow dews. It feels *great* to move—to charge her child's body with fresh air and sunshine like she is a plant that can photosynthesize.

She doesn't stop smiling until she reaches the top of the rock, mighty as any mountain. *Where to bury her? How to bury her? Why do we bother to bury at all?* Jane's toes feel below her until the rock bearing her weight splits, and a small chink opens. A tiny crevasse padded with muck and leaves. She uncups her hands to reveal the bird's organs crushed to jam. Bloodstains crease her palms, the color of squashed raspberries, but Jane is no longer terrified of blood, feathers, or flesh. She strokes the pile of feathers and bones as gently as Oma eventually learned to brush her coarse black hair at bedtime. Then, she lowers the hatchling into the open grave. She rakes mud, leaves, and tears over the corpse with her fingers. Jane marks the site using dried stems tied together into a cross. An urge to light incense like she's seen her mother do late at night when she can't sleep and thinks no one is watching comes over Jane. *Mother barricades herself in the Yellow Room, strikes a little bell, talks to photographs in Mandarin, and just cries and cries.*

Jane's mother doesn't know that her daughter watches her do this (she watches her do everything), so she believes that Jane doesn't know how to honor the dead or even the living like her mother's family does in the Asian way. But Jane *does* know. She knows much more about her parents' people and their clashing customs than her parents think. But she prefers to pray Nanny's way. Nanny comes from Brazil and believes in Jesus (but not like Oma, who goes to church). Nanny cleans for Jane's family on Sundays; she does not have time to attend church. Instead, when Jane's parents are screaming, Nanny comes into Jane's room and says, "Let's make *right here* our church," and teaches her to pray in her secret little way.

Dear Jesus/God, please give us all wings. Even Mommy and Daddy.
But especially this hatchling and Oma. And the man in black.
And maybe, someday, a little bit me. Amen.

"Amen! OK, kid, let's go! Hurry up!"

Jane slides down the rock pushing her hips side to side like a skier. A pigeon is disturbed by her path and takes flight. A candied nut vendor cooking a fresh batch sends his product's scent wafting on the wind. The sweet toasty smell climbs into Jane's nostrils and excites her for summer break, fireworks, and beach time. She forgets where she is and what she is doing for a moment. She forgets about funerals and frustrated fathers. She forgets everything except being a child whose grandma just died at the start of summer with her entire precious vacation still open before her. Jane windmills her arms as she races down the rock until strong arms catch her waist and lower her gently back to earth.

Once more, the man in black's large hand enfolds Jane's. He is indifferent to her dirty gravedigger's palms, and they fly from the park.

Parental tones crescendo on the oxblood stair. *How prettily and politely they speak to strangers!*

Jane straightens her back, stands, and waits, but the ghosts do not acknowledge her. They merely summon her obedience with their presence, and she trails after them, chin down, mute. The man in black rushes to open the door. Her mother takes no notice of the staff as she swoops into the back seat of the limousine. She is already pointing her back toward the funeral home and staring again at the cashmere across the street.

Jane lingers with her father and the bald funeral director on the curb. Another man in black, who is older, appears at the younger doorman's side. Together, they bolster the funeral home's front doors for Oma's mahogany coffin. As it goes by, Jane's father kisses it, but Jane does not. It's too far away, and she's too embarrassed to perch on tippy-toes and press her lips to the polished surface. She also worries that a maggot will pop out and dive down the back of her throat. Or she will slide face forward onto the coffin, causing the men in black to drop it. *Smash*! The lid will fly open, Oma's corpse will pop out like a jack-in-a-box, and everyone will scream. Her mother, shrillest of all.

Into the hearse's trapdoor swings the box. Daisies, lilies, and roses are heaped on top. Lilies remind Jane of Easter, reminding her of Oma, who loved all flowers and holidays—any excuse to consume candy and give presents to children.

Slap, slap, slap goes something down Madison Avenue. Jane looks down and sees grass blades sprouting between her toes.

My shoes! I left them behind in the park. There was no need to make a cross. Two patent headstones now mark the hatchling's grave ...

Jane's father wobbles toward her. As he almost trips, she does what she always sees her mother do when her father is stumbling around. She gets out of the way and tells herself, "It's just the heat."

The drunk father swoons closer, his breath sour as he grabs his daughter by the wrist *just a little too hard* and spins her around so that his cornflower eyes sear into her sesame ones. Tears gather but do not fall. Instead of shaking his child by the shoulders and yelling like he would if they were at home and her bed was found to be unmade or some other juvenile misdemeanor, he seizes Jane's hand, which she's balled into a fist, and pries it open. He does not notice the traces of raspberry red any more than he ever noticed the bittersweet fruits his mother shared with him from their little garden plot, which was once his when he was a child. Instead, he simply presses something shiny into Jane's palm.

"I think Oma wants you to have this. It was still pinned to the Austrian walking hat she always wore. I-I couldn't bear to put it in the ground. But don't tell your mother, or she'll sell it like she did the other one. My father bought my mother these brooches during a trip to Switzerland a long time ago, before I was even born. It must be strange for you to think about that. A time before not only you were born but also before me. She was the one who knew us both before we were us, and now she's … I don't know if I'm making any sense today, daughter. It does not matter. Now that both your grandparents are gone, I just wanted you to know that these bird brooches came as a pair, just like Oma and Opa."

Jane beams. She feels she has won something but doesn't know what or why as she pins Other Birdie to the inside of her black funeral dress and then covers the back of the golden needle piercing the fabric with her ropes of cinnamon-tinged black hair. The bird's pearl eyes push against her skin as she slides into the limousine beside her mother, donning humongous sunglasses and glaring out the tinted window. The gold metal is cool against the skin that covers Jane's heart.

Suddenly, Jane wants to know: "How come there's no church service for Oma?"

Her mother swipes off her oil-spill-sized sunglasses and bores her crow's eyes deep into Jane's pupils. "Because all of Oma's friends are either very old and still living in Europe or Argentina or dead."

Here, Jane's mother pauses and glances around furtively (to ensure no one is eavesdropping) before swiping the glasses back on. "Hitler didn't have anyone at his funeral either."

It takes only forty minutes to cross the Oma Bridge over the Hudson and reach the Bergen County Cemetery. This undulating green was converted into a burial ground from a golf course before Jane was born. Once, the golf course and the graveyard were reserved for "Whites only." When Jane's uncle, her father's little brother died, her father returned home drunk from the funeral, raving about the prime location of the family burial plot.

"One day, we'll all be buried in the Scott plot! You, Wing, me, and you, daughter, and maybe your kids one day a long time from now! Isn't that nice, family? We can stay together in this beautiful part of New Jersey forever. My father bought enough spots for all of us before he had the good sense to drop dead."

Jane's mother had recoiled and flushed mango.

"Not me!" she growled like a tiger. "In *my* country, we incinerate ourselves to ashes."

Jane is thinking about which family member she'd like to lie next to for all eternity and in what form when, suddenly, her mother screams. Jane cranes forward to see whether Oma's rotting skull has poked out from the casket and is now ogling us through the rearview window of the Cadillac hearse, but no. She is gone. They will bury her. They will bury Father, Mother, and, one day, even little Janey. Suddenly, Jane remembers Other Birdie. *The dragon, she knows.* One hand flies to her heart to protect the brooch, and the other balls into a fist—she is ready to fight her mother to keep the accessory, if necessary. But no, Jane's mother has not yet spotted her husband's treachery.

"Jesus, Wing! What is it now?"

"Look! Our little heathen escaped from the funeral parlor, lost her shoes, and ran around in the dirt! She can't walk around a cemetery with no shoes! It's indecent."

Jane's father says nothing. He turns away from his family, away from the hearse. His deadbolt falcon gaze goes through the windshield in rapt, predatory silence. The little procession has just entered the cemetery that has already swallowed his father and little brother. In another moment, it will also take his mother's body onto its tongue of dirt.

"No, Wing, she can't. After all, we're not in *your* country."

Carp

JUST AS THE LAST of the cherry blossoms darkened, the second day of Memorial Day Weekend arrived with the heat that bills itself as summer's official beginning. Sachiko, recently liberated from her twin careers as a freelance makeup artist and wife, dedicated her long weekend to watching her daughter's two dogs while she went hiking and microbrewery hopping upstate.

Her day started same as all the others. She boiled water for her matcha while she put on her uniform of all-black, applied minimal foundation and black eyeliner, then touched up her golden nail polish. A far cry from the rolling green of the rural prefecture where she had been raised, Sachiko believed that the city was no place for animals. *If this place is not fit for animals, what about humans*? She dismissed the thought as she dragged them, paws scorched on a furnace of asphalt, to the only appropriate place she could think of, Central Park.

All the rich and interesting residents, the people whose faces it had been her life's work to paint, had fled the city. As she made the journey from her one-bedroom on York Avenue, half the length of the island, toward the city's beating green heart, the Upper East Side was utterly deserted. This emptiness made her feel as though Manhattan commiserated with her abandonment. Husband, family, youth, industry—all could do without her now (unless there was some sort of emergency, then older women's wisdom was more than welcomed, it was required). Proximity and relevance were more closely linked than she'd ever realized.

The dogs panted the whole way but did their best to keep up. When their mistress dropped them at the strange apartment covered with black-and-white photos, they understood: *You are all we have now.* Sachiko was rather enjoying the canine company. Ever since her daughter had gone off to college, she'd not felt useful. The dogs' presence forced her to reimagine her routine. For instance, on their walk yesterday, they'd discovered a lovely, secluded creek babbling through the Ramble. There, the little trio promptly returned. The dogs immediately plunged their bodies into the cool tangle of water and stones. Sachiko wasted no time in slipping off her sandals and plunging her feet in. Ripples rinsed the emptiness between her toes, and pebbles pumiced her foot palms. This natural pedicure offered her something a little like joy.

She extracted a book about Tibetan Buddhism, her newest purchase from The Strand, from her Sunrise Mart canvas tote. Though she had been raised Nichiren (a religion she'd abandoned when marrying her agnostic ex), lately, Sachiko had been getting into the Vajrayana teachings. Her Japanese girlfriends made fun of her for cosplaying the midlife crises of their White lady counterparts.

"Soon, you'll be taking a new spiritual name and running off to India in search of enlightenment," they teased.

"At least it's better than sequined sweaters!"

Sachiko was old enough to laugh rather than give a shit. She'd learned from the naked faces of the world's most beautiful women that all outward appearances are meticulously constructed. No one knew anything, really, about anyone else—not even what they looked like, inside or out. This idea of not-knowing was baked into the premise of the spiritual teachings she was currently pursuing. Transformation made sense because it didn't. And, given the chaos of the last five or so years, that open acceptance and even embrace of contradiction was the only thing that really helped.

Of all the practices, the Vajra Dance was her favorite. After decades of hunching on a stool opposite some flinching model or actress, the slow, fluid gyrating of her hips and feet was a great joy. To call it "contemplation" and imagine herself dissolving energy blocks made the movement much more rewarding. The colorful mandala on which they danced reminded her of the parachute game her daughter had played in gym class as an elementary schooler—the one where the children lifted a rainbow-colored parachute over their heads before taking steps toward each other and crouching down so that the parachute creates a mushroom cloud around them. She never forgot how her daughter had squealed with delight when she emerged from that secret world of color, forbidden to parents.

Sachiko sank into her book, ready and willing to stay in that spot drenched by sunshine until she read her way to enlightenment when her daughter's terrier suddenly lunged into the water face-first. She saw what the dog was after—or, at least, she thought she did. Like a backward sunrise, a flicker of sunshine swimming crosstown, from East to West. *Could it be a carp? No, koi only live in corporate lobbies and the Brooklyn Botanical Gardens.* Since she was reading about contemplation, she tried not to suppress but instead follow her thoughts.

A carp's Latin namesake is carpere, *"to seize," itself derived from* καρπός, *the Greek word for fruit. There is also the Chinese story about the Dragon's Gate, where a legendary mountain promises dragonhood to any carp brave enough to make the final jump over the waterfall gushing from its side. According to that legend, however auspicious and mighty, every dragon is born of a lowly carp …*

Sachiko thought about sloshing after the fishy apparition and drew near the spot where the dog had first sensed it, the book still in hand. Somewhere inside echoed the author's discussion of shenpa, or hooks, emotional and spiritual.

Pema says Chögyam Trungpa taught her to try to vanish herself so that her body and mind were imprinted with the sky—rather than vice versa.

Sachiko wanted to embody this not-needing and was trying to let go of *needing to know* when a voice as stern as winter unexpectedly cut through.

"Excuse me, ma'am, but you're not allowed to be in that water. And your dogs need to be leashed at all times."

A frowning khaki-clad park ranger domed over her. Startled, Sachiko opened her palm in surprise. The book fell headlong into the water.

"Didn't you see the sign?"

"No, I didn't. I'm so sorry. But it's summer, and the dogs are just being dogs!"

"Think of it as a bath for all of New York City," the park ranger snapped back. "This is so much more than just some ordinary mountain stream. That's dirty water, taxpayer water."

Sachiko flushed beneath her sunglasses. Anger's flash rose, but neither woman claimed it.

"I'm a taxpayer too, you know," Sachiko managed as she dragged the dogs from the water.

"Aren't we all?"

Sachiko was so offended she forgot her book clinging to the bottom of the stream's basin, right where it fell. The ranger, whose job it was to protect the park from the city's inhabitants, didn't notice this act of defilement either.

The paperback lay there unnoticed all day and into the night, and the next morning. Its blue-sky cover depicted a flying bird. Distorted by the creek's alchemy of ripples and sun, the bird appeared to be soaring through a crystal instead of clouds.

A crowd gathered opposite the Boathouse at Bethesda, beneath the angel, on the lake's southern edge. Tourists around the terraces turned their heads away from their overpriced lunches toward the commotion. Sachiko and the dogs that were not hers were returning from the woods beyond the fountain like a renunciant renouncing renunciation comes down from his cave to make the town square his mandala. She did not even have to ask, "What is going on here?" because she could see the scene. *It's Memorial Day Weekend, and a Brown man from Queens or some other outer borough is fishing in the light blue lake in the very expensive heart of the city where tourists from Europe and China are busy rowing and taking wedding pictures.* The circled-up onlookers—locals and visitors alike— heaved around him in fascination. They struggled to get their phones closer to his line, wriggling with a life about to be extinguished hooked on the end. *Death in the afternoon, how unexpected and exciting!* Everyone descended into the violence of the poor man's sport, known as his dinner. They wanted to know: Will this modest fisherman put his catch back or keep his kill?

Whatever was hooked there, meanwhile, bitterly resisted its end. The fisherman's back was aimed at Sachiko and the dogs. She could see that he was clad in a faded Mets T-shirt as he continued to twist his torso. A patch of sweat the size of a congratulatory handprint spread visibly across the back of his T-shirt. After the building of quiet suspense came a pull and a push. Finally, a small cry escaped his lips. The crowd became a circle that contracted, leaning in to witness the gold-orange flash that suddenly broke the water's surface. Like the sun setting upside down in the East, it rose entirely into the golden-sunshine-filled air before disappearing from view.

"Let's see him!" a woman with a French accent called out, her thumb hovering over the video record button on her phone.

The fisherman obliged this best new director from Canal +, causing the studio audience to erupt into primetime cheers. All Sachiko could register of the carp as it came flying out of the water were its big black eyes. They reflected nothing of herself, only the fish's horror. She gazed at its lips and saw that the fish's breath was not ours. She did not turn away from its fading orange mouth as it moved with the frantic motion of her daughters' dogs' noses, searching the muddy earth for smells.

Poor old carp! He ought to have been safe in those conservatory waters! Dirty, taxpayer waters ...

The longer Sachiko watched the fish drown on dry land, the more she felt confident that the carp was not a fish but a dying sage entreating her. It was a hermeneutics of helplessness as the fish seemed to Sachiko to cry out again and again. For the briefest moment, she read the mystery of our burning sun written upon the fish's lips, unmediated by a blank page of water. Seconds that felt like months passed until Sachiko began to understand what the carp did the minute the hook went in. The fisherman had no intention of putting the fish back. And it would take a very long time (in fish time) for the fish to die.

When the true end was near, Sachiko simply could not take it anymore. She thought of her child in pain and exited, then led the dogs around the fountain where the bronze statue of an angel leaned forward, pointing her iron wings obliquely to heaven. Like her, Sachiko turned her back to the fisherman and her face toward the gospel singers sounding Ave Maria's beneath a tiled archway. Dark magenta cherry blossoms surrendered from their trees swirled underfoot. To their tune of glory, she circumambulated the fountain slowly in the hopes of remaking her mandala. She prayed the whole time: "Please, Lord Buddha, make all the world vegan and stop the overfishing/murders of the ocean." But only the gospel singers' faint alleluias echoed back.

When she reached the mandala's center, the fish was dead. The fisherman was posing for pictures with the carp's glistening corpse. The fish's body turned slowly, like a hanged man in the gallows of his executioner's arms. Suddenly, a mental prompt came upon her as if faxed by some disembodied Rinpoche: *Study the man, not the corpse.* The fish killer appeared Dominican and middle-aged. She didn't know many Latino people and had only been to Mexico once. It was the '90s, when her daughter was tiny, and they'd gone to Cozumel as a family to swim with the dolphins. In California, she knew, Mexicans and Koreans overlapped quite a bit. Something about that was pertinent to the history of the race riots. But all of it happened before Sachiko moved to the US, and no one had ever told her any of that history.

The fisherman's tennis shoes were as worn in and dated as his denim shorts, and he carried a small white cooler, the coffin icebox into which he placed the carp when the wriggling had mostly ceased. The fact that he had the cooler with him made it clear that the man intended to take home, grill, then eat whatever he caught in the park that day. In plain view of all, though none noticed, a tear rolled down Sachiko's cheek in judgment of her judgment. Not because of shenpa, but because a poor man far from his country came to the rich people's park to fish. It reinforced her understanding that suffering as a sport was simply the way of the world. How was the suffering of the man or the fish or even the tourists gleefully filming it all any different from her marriage, her career, and her daughter's childhood ending?

One moment, the carp was here, swimming around in his pond of ignorant bliss. The next moment, he was gone.

Monday evening, her daughter texted from upstate: "Missed my train! I'm gonna be a little later than planned. So sorry, Mom!"

While they waited, Sachiko and the dogs fell asleep on the couch. Her dream returned her to the water. This time, she was carrying nothing but the unhooked dogs' leashes. Without her restraining them, they gleefully raced down the slope toward the little creek. But before the dogs could fling their bodies into the cool, moving waters, Sachiko was mindful of the ranger and went to leash their enthusiasm. She drew their powerful, leaping bodies back from the water, and they weaved along the little shore both ways, laughing up and downstream. When they'd had their fill, the dogs followed Sachiko away from the water and shook the brook off their coats so the cool droplets rained down on her. The three of them piled together on a mossy patch of the riverbank. Sachiko stroked their ears while peering absentmindedly into the tiny eddies breaking up the current.

Suddenly, the terrier lunged. Sachiko saw what she was after at once—or, at least, she thought she did, but no, the book was long gone. Washed away or taken, whether by human or animal or simply disintegrated, there was no way to tell. The terrier's nose turned up just one solitary page in the mud. To please Sachiko because she loved her, the dog hooked it with its teeth and hauled the sheet onto the riverbank. Though the paper was half-dissolved, Sachiko's annotations were still visible, if not legible. She tried to decipher a phrase marked with an asterisk, thinking she should reach for a piece of paper to jot down what was essential and should not be forgotten. But there was an interruption before she could—a sound at the door.

Her daughter was panting in the hall with creases under her eyes while the smell of pasta cooking wafted around them. A canvas tote filled with farm stand vegetables shifted awkwardly in her arms.

"Mom, I'm *so* sorry!"

Mother and daughter did not hug. They never did. Her daughter hovered awkwardly in the hallway while Sachiko reached for the leash, but before she could catch either dog, they both catapulted out of the apartment into their mother's arms. For a moment, Sachiko was terrified. For the last three nights, she'd had company. She was afraid to be alone and began reaching for her shoes.

"Want me to walk you to the subway?"

"Nah, it's late. I've got an Uber coming in two minutes. Here, I got all these fresh veggies for you. We stopped at this cute farm stand on the way back. Maybe I can come by tomorrow after work. We can grill them up with some fish?"

Her daughter looked tired. Her daughter's dogs were exhausted. Everybody was ready to go home, except Sachiko, who was home already, except this wasn't her "home," just the space she was paying all her monies to occupy now. She accepted the vegetables with faked gratitude, then closed the door.

The next evening after work, the daughter arrived at her mother's apartment, craving teriyaki salmon. Upon reaching the building door, the dogs stiffened their legs and refused to move.

"Don't worry," cooed the daughter. "Mommy's not abandoning you for another weekend. We're just here to have dinner with your Oba-chan."

They both made cow eyes at her and whined and whined while she buzzed up. When no answer came, the daughter texted her mother impatiently. No reply. Clouds began forming overhead as a storm blew in. The heavens suddenly gushed white showers of rain while lightning shuttled in the sky. Cherry blossoms whipped up by the wind swirled all the way to York

Avenue from their trees in Central Park. The daughter was just marveling at the dance of pink petals in the rain when a young couple around her age exited the building under a single umbrella. They held the door out for the drenched daughter and her dogs without a thought.

Up the narrow flights they climbed, five long stories, but her mother was not in the apartment. The normally immaculate studio was in complete disarray with clothes ripped from the closet, papers whirlpooling on the living room floor, and the vegetables she'd brought over yesterday spilled all over the kitchen counter. An empty sake bottle listed in the sink. The place was dark and silent, except for the sound of running water and amber light spilling from the bathroom. The terrier, the bolder of the two dogs, approached the bathroom door with her nose low, sniffing. She pawed at the yellow crack, simpered, and then barked.

With trembling hand, the daughter rapped on the bathroom door.

"Mom? Are you in there?"

No answer. The door was not locked, so she pushed it open. Her dogs did not follow.

"Mom?" she called again.

The bath was running with the drain open. A wooden masu was perched on the edge of the bath, next to the conditioner. All the lights blazed, even the little makeup lamp suctioned to the wall. The medicine cabinet was ripped from the wall. Its contents, her mother's makeup, the tools of her trade, was littered all over the floor. Where the mirrored cabinet had once hung over the sink, a small hole to the east now opened through the building's exoskeleton. She peered out and gasped. Between the buildings and the clouds, knitted together by raindrops swirling with dark pink cherry blossoms, her eyes caught the faint image of a hundred-foot-long dragon. It was black all over and rising straight up over the East River, its golden talons flashing.

Years later, when the daughter became a mother herself and entered therapy because her husband threatened to divorce her if she did not, she told her therapist: "After that Memorial Day Weekend, I never saw her again. My dad said it was 'just like her' to up and vanish into thin air. He said that's why he left. But he didn't know her like I did. My mom loved me— she would never abandon me like that. Everyone thinks I'm crazy, but I swear to you, I *did* see it. I did. All-powerful. Terrifying. Divine. Black all over except for golden talons flashing—it was my mother, the Dragon God."

No English

918 URIS. OLDER MALE. Chinese ethnic origin. Daughter refused visit from rabbi/priest, saying, "Religion is backward," despite request for pastoral care. Likely miscommunication (no English).

Rabbi's plum-colored Post-It fluttered in the air-conditioning, stuck to the ancient conference phone. The antiquated communication device dated to the pre-9/11 era and occupied a disproportionate share of the small, chipped laminate desk allotted to interns in the pastoral care office. None of the interns liked answering that phone. The first time it had rung during their training, the young, newly minted cantor had picked it up absent-mindedly.

"Hello, pastoral care. This is Eli?"

Immediately, uber-Jewish Eli was summoned to the maternity floor on six to baptize a dead Catholic baby and then spiritually anesthetize its collapsing parents, who believed sin, not God, had caused their baby's premature death. As I said, none of the interns liked answering that phone.

Mathematically speaking, 50 percent of the patients admitted to the hospital in Manhattan these days enter their religion as "none." However, enough still asked to see the priest, rabbi, or part-time imam. But it was not every day that Candice, the designated atheist on the pastoral care staff, got a request. She convinced herself that the rabbi wasn't sending her to 918 Uris because she was "some sort of Asian" but because he knew how much she hated praying. He was doing her a favor by rerouting her from the usual morning's duties at the bedside of Christian/Jewish/Muslim heart attack survivors.

Few souls think to ask for spiritual counsel without asking for God. Usually, Rabbi dispatched

Candice to the bedside of "challenging" patients. Because she was young. Because she was female, which meant patient. Also, her father was an addict, so she knew how to sit with the detoxing and not be rattled by their ghosts.

As Rabbi and others liked to remind her, despite her lack of formal clerical training, her mere presence was usually enough to put all sorts of the apathetic and dying or despondent and critically ill (especially older single men) at ease. Her friends with parent-pleasing professions didn't understand. They disparaged her early thirties career pivot to a helping profession over Sunday dim sum.

"What happened to graphic design?"

"It's a shame you've stopped doing design. That logo you did for that thingamajig was so cool."

"My mom's sister's husband works at McKinsey, and I hear they're always looking for reliable creatives. Want me to connect you?"

She did not. At least, not in that way. Perhaps it was her past, but Candice had aged emotionally apart from her peers for whatever reason. She felt her trajectory to be as ancient as a primordial dragon, hoarding whatever treasure came her way and hiding her weak spot. She went through life from subway stop to subway stop as if commuting between alternate dimensions. For ten years now, she'd been sleepwalking through the millennia of her youth.

Candice fidgeted with the name badge swinging from her lanyard for the first forty minutes of her shift and ruminated on the summons to China. She'd never been, even though countless unnamed cousins lived there. Her pathetic Mandarin was worrisome. As soon as she opened her mouth, it always gave her away. She pretended she wasn't procrastinating, a humiliation Rabbi would never understand, by reviewing and re-reviewing the census for her floors and lingering over the last of her Starbucks. Even that, like her Chineseness, was a lie. Really, she was waiting for Joe, due any minute for his morning prayers. The handsome surgical nurse was the only Muslim employee she'd encountered in the hospital. Every day, multiple times a day, Joe came to the pastoral care office searching for a private place to worship. And Candice often just happened to be there.

Today, she longed to see him more than usual. Joe was attractive, American-born, a convert. Along with the broadness of his back and smile, that, she was forced to admit, was part of the attraction. Inside-outsiders both, he understood. As if on cue, Joe appeared and greeted Candice with his crescent moon smile.

"Morning, chappy!"

The delicate ridges rippling under his eyes indicated he was midway through another grueling double shift. Candice wasn't sure if he loved his work or made it seem that way to kick the can on the question of grabbing a drink sometime. If he never left the hospital, he wasn't not asking her out because he didn't like her—he simply didn't have the time.

She enjoyed watching Joe bend over to root around in the cupboards underneath the bookcase loaded with Gideon Bibles in English and Spanish. Beneath the paperbacks rested a handful of Chinese editions and a few bilingual Korans. Joe blew a kiss to the row of Koran spines before reverently removing one of the polyester prayer rugs stacked in the cupboard below. Rabbi kept them there for Muslim patients, just in case.

"Morning, Joe," was all Candice could manage stupidly before diverting her eyes from the muscular nurse's scrubbed form.

He stared at her in a non-creepy way, but she refused to return the look for fear of her mother, who remained embedded in her inner ear like a rent-controlled tenant despite being on the opposite coast.

"Marry White, daughter!" came the wisdom of Calabasas. "And do it fast. Asian men are trouble. They keep you down all your life, then die early."

Even though Candice's mother had said nothing about non-White, non-Asian men, the answer was so obvious that the question didn't even need to be posed. The Chinese-dominant neighborhood where she had been raised was fiercely racist. Her neighbors were full of adverse ideas about their neighbors. Overwhelmingly, they were against Blacks, Latinos, Arabs, American Indians, Japanese, Vietnamese,

Filipinos, Chinese from the "wrong" (i.e., Cantonese-speaking) parts of China, expats, and anyone who'd ever set foot in Taiwan. In "good" first-generation communities, excitement and especially Blackness were not allowed. All these faux freedoms belonged to a fake future propagated by White people to keep the non-White people in line. Unspoken cultural expectations delayed her life's gratification and clashed with the codes of her country. Ultimately, these external pressures converged with her parents to construct the restrictive container in which she grew up like glass eels netted in Western eddies and raised in concrete pens before being shipped to Asia.

Maybe that's why Candice was here, with her huge black eyes and flat, transparent body. Confusion about what delineated "native waters" had instilled in her an unshakable urge to break open the life-cycle loop. An uninvited visitor from an alien world, she was a trained graphic designer lurking around the hospital and trying to become a chaplain without going to divinity school or becoming a priest. Thrashing through captivity in an attempt to mature spontaneously had so far proven impossible—it remained in her genes to parasitize the excitement of others. Her acupuncturist friend, a

Texas blond, once told her: "A seedling buried in an underground parking lot will grow through any chink in the concrete, bending every way it has to, to break through and sip the sky." Candice was neither tree nor concrete parking garage ceiling. She was respectful, which meant being whatever those around her with higher status wanted her to be.

Watching her friends go off to confirmation or bar mitzvahs, she'd come to believe that being installed early on with religious software was simpler than being brought up atheist. At least you could blame entities for your faults and ask for forgiveness. In Candice's household, everything from the rain to the raccoons was her fault. While she believed this propensity to blame was cultural, tantamount to the callousness of the Chinese, she also knew this to be untrue. Her dad had died when she was in elementary school. The death of the immigrant patriarch so early in the uprooting process had left the family rudderless, adrift. What little Mandarin they'd spoken in the home so the kids could learn English had stopped immediately. Candice could order dinner at a restaurant and ask where the bathroom was, but that was about it. Her mother's

English wasn't excellent, either, but it got her by and protected mother and daughter from having intimate discussions that probed too deeply into the past. Her younger brother advanced quickly through school, double majored in econ and French, and thus served as the family's official interface with America. The family always celebrated Memorial Day and the Fourth of July, but never Qingming. No rice wine was ever offered to their dead father's grave. No thoughts given to the karma of perpetuating yet another generation of restless ghosts. Except the images never fully dissipated. Again and again, the funeral parlor people came for the gelatinous body, every hour more transparent with its thin layer of muscle tissue barely concealing the ceased organs, all reduced in size save one. The smell of formaldehyde in the living room. The ceaseless aquatic glow of the television, perpetually glued to the news, that never, ever switched off.

As for what had killed her father, the family never mentioned it in any language.

The sexy nurse lowered himself into an east-facing corner. The broad muscles of his back flexed beneath a thin layer of scrubs in the just-right light that poured in through the unwashed windows.

Candice knew he knew she was watching him pray. They both enjoyed it. She pushed her mother from her mind, wondering what it would feel like for him to take her in his arms and rock her torso the way he now rocked his. Salinity from somewhere (her morning bagel?) coated the inside of her cheeks.

When he was done, she let him walk her to the elevator to start her rounds.

"Well, this is it. I go down. You go up."

It was not an innuendo, but it made her blush anyway.

On nine, the nurse's station resembled a giant magnet in a cartoon. Aggressively oblong, it suctioned papers, people, flowers, food—everything—to itself. Behind it stooped a bored young woman with a body shaped like a capital G. She was built like a willow tree with acrylic nails professionally decorated, each with a different astrological sign. Candice recognized her but clocked her name tag to make sure.

"Hey, Michaela. How's it going?"

Michaela shot her a look that said, *I changed the linens and lines for a thousand assholes this morning and have three screaming kids at home.* She glanced at Candice's nametag, then her head-to-toe J. Crew outfit, and frowned.

"And who are you again?"

Candice smiled. She was used to not being remembered. She tried never to take it personally, especially when a White person confused her with another random Asian girl. But Michaela wasn't White.

"I'm the chaplain intern assigned to this floor. Rabbi sent me to visit with Mr. West. He said the patient's not religious but wanted a chaplain anyway ..."

"Mister Who?"

"918 Uris."

"Oh, him. The rich old Chinese guy? I happen to have his chart right here. Hmm, let's see. He's just had surgery to biopsy a tumor in his stomach. Tsk, tsk, malignant. Still, notes say it went as well as it could. Now we're just waiting for him to pass gas, then he can go home. Oh, and when you go in, there is an adult daughter. I don't think she's married. Goes by Ms. West. She's very nice and speaks English well enough. I think they're planning to do chemo in Brooklyn, where the patient lives with his wife. The wife, by the way, has yet to appear."

The information streamed from her mouth into Candice's ears like plankton. But it was not enough to assuage her anxiety. She needed more.

"Do you know why he requested someone from pastoral care? Is he having a hard time coping with his diagnosis?"

"How should I know? He doesn't speak a damn word of English!"

Michaela was done speaking. She buried her face in a file and pointed vaguely toward 918.

Mr. West occupied one of the cushier corner suites at the end of the hall. These large suites were normally reserved for hospital donors, second-tier VIPs, and retired attendings who'd fallen ill. The east-facing room received the sunrise bouncing off the river via the backs of marigold taxis instead of the coveted, lush green Park Avenue view. Sunlight poured in. It spotlighted the pillows and disarrayed sheets heaped atop the chair by the window, rumpled evidence that someone had camped there overnight.

The patient himself was awake and alert in his carefully tied hospital gown. His body was positioned between a battery of pillows. Propped ninety degrees upright in the bed, he was utterly absorbed in watching CNN on an iPad in a Louis Vuitton case. A stack of Mandarin newspapers rose atop his otherwise tidy rolling table.

His chin briefly lifted when Candice entered, but his eyes remained immovable. Because of her gender and his age, this interaction was appropriate.

"Hello," said Candice to the air. Head slightly bowed, hands clasped in front of her waist, and, most importantly, no eye contact. "I'm Candice from pastoral care. Do you mind if I visit with you for a little while?"

The daughter the nurse had spoken of paced beside the windows on the father's other side. At first, Candice failed to notice her. The light coming in was so bright that the sunshine almost entirely washed out the woman's little silhouette. Seeing a person with a badge, but no white coat, Ms. West hurried to the foot of the bed and demanded, "Huh? I'm sorry, who you?"

"I'm the chaplain. From pastoral care."

"What that? Like social worker?"

"I visit patients and their families to see how they are doing emotionally and spiritually. I'm also here to pray with you if you like. Or just listen."

Ms. West's reply was a look Candice knew well from watching her mother attempting to do math in English. A cocktail of shock, disdain, and pain. The man in the bed ignored everything, especially the women. He kept giggling as if the news anchors were stand-up comedians. Candice got on with it.

"May I ask how you two are related?"

"No, no! Not!"

Ms. West waved her hands about when she spoke. Shame flashed in Candice's cheeks, though she knew what the woman meant: *He's my father, not my husband.* However, pointing this out early in the interaction might embarrass her. Candice knew what to do.

"I'm sorry ..." she began, forgetting what came next.

The slim jadeite bangle in pale lavender dangling around Ms. West's slender wrist distracted her. It caught the pale morning rays commingled with hospital lighting and illuminated. Before he died, Candice's father had given her one just like it. "This belonged to your great-grandma in China," he'd mumbled while sundowning. The words had come out in garbled Mandarin, so her aunt had translated: "Purple jade is the rarest and luckiest. Wear it and remember me."

Naturally, Candice never wore it. She was terrified of getting bumped on the subway, banging her wrist against the handrail and shattering it into more particles than her father's cremated body. Even though Candice respected her aunt, the woman was full of unresolved trauma from her childhood in the mountains of Yunnan. Their family was a conspiracy, and the aunt was a key operator. Whenever relatives interpreted other relatives for her, Candice felt that something essential was lacking, left out deliberately. Her lack of Mandarin, therefore, simultaneously endangered and protected her from whatever nuclear secrets her family was hiding.

"That's a beautiful bracelet," Candice finally awkwardly managed. "Purple jade is the rarest and luckiest."

Ms. West did not smile. She rubbed the bracelet with her right thumb and forefinger.

"OK. You stay. Nice to meet you, Miss Chapman."

"Nice to meet you, too."

Candice bowed her head a little, and Ms. West bowed back. Both women glanced again at the man in the bed. Again, he ignored them.

"How is he doing today?"

"OK. Better than yesterday."

"That's good to hear." Candice pointed to the sheets crumpled on the reclining chair. "And how are *you* doing?"

Ms. West moved her eyes away like too much direct contact was hurting her.

"OK, OK."

She stared out the window, fixed on a pigeon. The bird carefully stepped around the spikes installed on the long sill to ensure none of its kind ever nested there.

Candice stepped closer to the man in the bed, politely ignoring him.

"You look tired, ma'am. Did you sleep here?"

"Yes, Miss Chapman, I am very tired. I sleep here every night now for more than one week. At least eighteen hours a day, I stay in this hospital. Come from near Long Island. Go home and shower. Come back again. Yes, very tired. It's very hard to come here."

"Those are very long days! It sounds like you have a lot on your plate. I'm sorry. I didn't catch how you know Mr. West …"

"I'm his daughter!"

"Oh, I see. I apologize. I didn't realize. Does he speak any English?"

"No English."

"You have to translate for him?"

She nodded.

"No wonder you're exhausted! It must be difficult to be here night and day, translating and worrying. Do you have other relatives who also come to help?"

Ms. West shook her head with a thrashing motion. "No one. Yes, it is very difficult to be here all the time. My mom cannot come. She too old to sit on a train for an hour alone."

"She must be very worried about him, your mom."

"Not really," laughed Ms. West. The sound was far away, almost healthy. "They both old. They had nice life together. She just doesn't like to stay alone, so my husband and son check on her."

The silence that opened permitted Candice to recall something her mother had said when she'd first relayed her intent to study end-of-life pastoral care. They were on FaceTime, and Candice had been sitting nicely at her desk in a button-up shirt while her mother had been glazing her fresh-caught dinner with sweet-salty sauce. *In the West, people obsessed with death. That's why they no talk. If you not being sad about death, you a monster with no feelings. A saucy-oh-path, right? In the East, it not like that. We always think about death. Not being sad can make you Buddha.*

As if she could hear the maternal subway announcer in Candice's brain, Ms. West's face stayed tender for two or three minutes, but her lip corners curled into something of a sneer when she noticed the device in her father's lap. He was watching CNN in English and pretending to be engaged. With the practiced stern gentleness that belongs to the mothers of small children, she prized the tablet away from her elderly father. He grunted a little but allowed it. Without a word, Ms. West searched for a Chinese news channel, turned up the volume, then returned the tablet to him. The old man smiled the half-moon smile of grandfathers and emperors, then was immediately reabsorbed in the news of impending global financial implosion.

Once, not long after their father died, the aunt had imposed on the house dressed in a sequined animal-themed sweater with red glasses pinching the end of her nose. She opened the door without knocking and looked around.

"Where is your mother?"

Their mother was not at home. They had no idea where she'd gone or when she'd be back. The aunt immediately set about cooking a week's worth of dinner to stash in recycled takeout containers in the freezer.

"Tell me what is going on. How is school?"

"I have a science report due tomorrow," Candice's brother confessed, "but I haven't started."

"What is the topic?"

"Agriculture or something."

"How fortunate!" While she chopped, boiled, and grilled, the aunt promptly launched into a long lecture about the grand history of eels. "You know, back in China, our family made a small fortune harvesting eels. For many, many generations, we were eel people. Your great-great-grandfather was famous for knowing all the secret spots where the tastiest ones hang out. You see, the flavor lies in understanding the secrets of migration. Glass eels are famous for leaving the coastal areas of their birth to explore ten thousand rivers and streams, overcoming all sorts of challenges. They may look frail, but they are actually super powerful."

Something fishy was boiling in a pot. She lidded it, glanced at her watch, and pulled up a video on the Internet. It was a decade old, in Chinese, without subtitles. The children pretended to watch, though their eyes were on CNN flickering on mute in the background.

"You see? Look how they drag themselves over strange, wet grass and burrow through sands to get to headwaters and into ponds. Crazy, right?"

"What if they can't make it? Do they just die?" Candice remembered asking. Or was it her brother who asked?

The aunt shook her head. "No. If this strategy fails, they instinctively band together. They pile up their bodies by the tens of thousands and use each other to climb over obstacles, even vertical walls. This way, they colonize everything, reaching even the tiniest creeks."

The water in the pot almost boiled over. The lid came off. The aunt stirred, then strained, talking all the while.

"The young eels' diet changes in the fresh, new water. They gorge themselves on little crabs, worms, and other insects not found in their native waters. Their bodies grow. They change from clear, completely see-through to a kind of golden color. During this stage of life, they are renamed 'yellow eels.'"

She declared this proudly, only to realize she'd lost her audience. The aunt stood up suddenly, crossed the small room, and turned off CNN for the first time the children could remember. They gaped at their brazen relative, who carried on as if nothing unusual had happened.

"Every July, the switch of instinct flips. The eels are suddenly called home. They cross the wetlands at night to begin their trip across the open ocean back to their spawning grounds. However, their guts dissolve when they leave their temporary continent, making feeding impossible. They rely on stored energy like one set of batteries, their eyes grow humongous, and their bodies revert to their old, transparent selves. They turn silvery on the sides, and the mix of yellow and clear hides them from sharks and other enemies. Nobody knows exactly how they do it or why they travel so far, but we call these ones 'big eyes.'"

The aunt finished cooking and speaking at the same time. She was so pleased with herself. Both children nodded, pretending to be fascinated. Really, they were just hungry. All talk of eels dissolved as they slurped the steaming noodles and hugged their aunt goodbye.

Candice's brother wrote his report later that night in the parentless apartment. He handed it in the next day and received an A. It was titled "Cattle Ranching in California: An Overview."

Ms. West must have been in her late fifties. Her body was mature but still small, like an American preteen, no more than 150 centimeters long. Streaks of silver raked her hair. It was graying more from the sides than the roots. Her black eyes were undeniably huge and grew huger as she started talking.

"My parents moved to the US after me, almost thirty years now. In China, my father was engineer, but here, he fixes things in buildings. Handyman no life for him, but he never learn English, so what can you do? There are many differences between home and here, so many things have changed, and they never really feel at home in American culture. But my son is born here, like you. He only child, now thirty. A lawyer. Unmarried. You married?'"

Candice knew how to respond. "A lawyer! Goodness. You must be *very* proud."

Ms. West nodded, though they both knew she never told *him* that. "Yes, hmmm. You married?"

The golden rule of chaplaincy was *never* to disclose anything personal. Keep the focus on the patient. *The patients are our teachers. The patients are our teachers.* And yet.

"No, I'm not married."

"Oh." Ms. West's face fell, showing its many slender frown lines.

"But don't worry! I have a serious boyfriend in his third year of medical school." The frown lines melted into a small smile. "Please, tell me more about your family. Do you still have relatives back home?"

Ms. West was unused to being the focus of an interview (especially in English), so she quickly tired of it and changed the subject. She wanted to know (and it wasn't a question), "So, where are you *from.*"

Again, Candice knew how to respond. "I was born here, but my parents are from China. All our family is still there, except my grandparents, who have all passed."

Ms. West grinned. Her tone changed, with the voice going up a little.

"Oh! I see, I see! But you don't speak Chinese? Why no?"

This one, Candice still did not know how to answer. She shook her head, embarrassed. *Because my friends who went to Chinese school got made fun of and beat up for practicing characters on graph paper during math class. Because I have no desire to be "competitive" or work in finance. Because Father died when I was young, and Mother couldn't handle it—three kids, two languages, no husband or in-laws— all on her own. Because I was desperate to be blond with big boobs and blue eyes so the soccer boys—or any boys other than the Asian fetish weirdos—would want me.*

She felt too ashamed to reveal to a stranger-patient that she had a dead dad. Not because he was dead (all fathers eventually die), but because he had died poor in the West before he could complete his American success story.

"I studied Spanish at school. They told me it would be more useful in my career."

No English was needed to interpret the subtext. Ms. West smiled the smile of courtesan mothers.

"That's OK, you still a good girl! I study a little Spanish, too, long time ago. So we have the same education. Back home we care for the sick. Care for our parents. You a very good girl, care for other people's parents. Your mother must be proud of you."

"Yes. It is our duty to take care of elders." *This is getting too personal.* Candice needed to get the conversation off her and back on the patient. "Has your father just had surgery?"

Ms. West nodded and dropped her voice to a conspiratorial whisper. "They found cancer. But he doesn't know. We don't tell him. He almost ninety, why tell? It would just upset him. You know. We have the same education."

"I understand," said Candice, but she didn't.

She had so many questions. Was it legal not to tell a human being that doctors have discovered an enormous malignancy growing inside them that will slowly, eventually kill them? Did the patient know he was terminal, but everyone pretended otherwise for the daughter/wife's benefit? Why lie like that to the people you love most? Candice knew that her people were more afraid of fearing fear than dreaded events coming to pass. They believed in the power of energies, interconnected thought forms, and qi. To think about death leads to speaking about death, which leads to its manifestation, or karma. *Train your mind to focus on the positive. Ignore the unpleasant. Carry on with your day, which is as good a day as any to die.*

"When he goes home, will he continue treatment?"

The arm with the jade bangle reached out and seized Candice's wrist. The breach was physically aggressive, as if rude fingers could communicate what polite speech could not. Namely, *are you insane? Don't you have eyes to see that this is my dad DYING here?*

Candice was confused. She thought the daughter had reached the acceptance stage. But no, she was still hauling her thin, flat body across hostile wetlands. Her desperation was starting to leak through.

Candice wanted to help because that was her job. But in a situation such as this, what does "help" actually mean? She asked the only question she could think of without projecting.

"Will you be the one looking after him?"

"Of course. But he won't know."

Candice tried to retrieve her arm, but Ms. West wasn't done talking. She had the floor now, perhaps for the first time in years. She clutched on to Candice's arm like it was a karaoke microphone.

"It is like this, Miss Chapman. Women take care of parents and in-laws. It's always like this. Women take care of inside the house, men outside. But you know, my generation is tired. We take care of children, our parents, and if our children have children. I quit my job a long time ago to take care of my son. But he is a good boy. He comes to visit his grandpa. I don't mind, it is proper, but I don't know about the next generation. My son's generation. Will he look after his parents?"

It was then that Candice deduced what the woman wanted from her. Ms. West's primary worry was not that her father would die and leave her bereft but that her son would be too far removed from his grandfather when he did die to see how it would one day be his duty to help his mother die with similar dignity (or marry a traditionally minded Asian girl who would do it). Ms. West was afraid of herself, of her eel-like body aging in a culture hostile to aging female bodies, alone without parents or siblings. If the purpose of immigrant life was to swim far, explore the world's crannies, and try to go home to die well, then dying awkwardly and unfamiliarly, far from home, was the ultimate failure. What Ms. West wanted from Candice was what every patient or their family members facing a terminal diagnosis wanted: assurance where none was possible.

Their arms were still intertwined. Candice thought of her aunt's juvenile eels, piling up their bodies to get to a new life, no matter the cost.

"It's hard living far away from home in a culture that is so different," she began gently. "Traditional customs and values are not lost … but everywhere, things are changing. I know for me growing up in this country, I learned by watching my mom. I saw how she did her duty as a daughter, so even though I grew up in America, when my dad got sick, I learned to do mine. You said your son comes and visits his grandpa so he sees how you care for your father. I am sure, when the time comes, he will be there for you too."

Her broad face relaxed. The lips curled into a grin huge enough to match her straining eyes. She let go of Candice's arm and clutched her hand instead. Ms. West's fingers were bony and almost transparent at the knuckles. Nonetheless, warmth flowed through her skin.

"Yes, yes! Thank you! You are right. My son is a good boy. And you are a good girl. But it really is hard—such a different culture. Things like toilet paper are so expensive here. I feel—I feel cheated. Elders are not given respect. But our life has been good here. He went to a good college. All on scholarship. Good law school. He works hard like you work hard. We get good things when we work hard."

Once loosened, Ms. West's tongue flowed with the ferocious audacity of mud season creeks. Their intimacy was approaching the maximum, but Rabbi would want to know where Candice directed that emotional outflow. Her work was not done.

"May I ask if you are religious?"

The humongous eyes blinked. Something like incredulity rippled through Ms. West's inky pupils. She looked almost hurt, like she'd taken shelter in the eddy only to end up in some hostile net.

"No. No religion. My grandma was not religious. She said, 'Just be good, and you will get good back.' Simple. Since my grandma was not religious, she did not teach me and my brothers, so I am not. These things come through the family. Maybe my great-grandma was Buddhist. Yes, she was definitely Buddhist. What about you? Was your grandmother Buddhist or Christian?"

"One of each, I believe. But I'm not sure. My mother never talks about these things."

Candice had been in 918 Uris for almost an hour. The time had come to pray or go away. She needed to signal pastoral authority and skillfully redirect the visit before leaving.

"In that case, perhaps I can offer you a blessing, Ms. West? Good wishes for your father's health and you during this difficult time?"

"That's OK, Miss Chapman. But you can think of us later and light some incense. That would be nice. Thank you, Miss Chapman, for visiting us. I enjoyed talking to you."

"Likewise. Thank you for sharing with me. Be well."

For the first and only time, Candice dared to look directly at Mr. West and smiled. This time, he looked at her too. He grinned a little, so she bowed to him slightly. The elder nodded. Snow-streaked tendrils fell across his eyes, but he did not brush them away. He smiled wider and wider like he'd understood every word. It was true—he had very little English, but no English was necessary for Mr. West to know that he was dying from cancer and that his adult daughter was commanding everyone in the hospital (including his wife) to hide it from him. He did not need to know English to know she was doing this because she loved him.

He had crossed the vast ocean to be with his daughter and grandson despite his paternal failings. He had brought his wife, the now grown girl's mother, to this country and spent his savings to help his grandson get the Western education he needed to regain previous generations' lost wealth. His flat, yellow body had changed, then changed again. Now it was dissolving into transparent gelatin, of which, soon, nothing would remain except ash.

Through it all, his daughter had remained filial. What a success story! He was dying, yes, dying far from his country. She was his only child in the West, a retired seamstress who'd raised a lawyer, and a "good girl." Even though he'd rather die than tell her this, he was very proud.

Normally, Candice and Joe intersected at least one more time during the workday. Usually in the late afternoon, before he changed out of his teal scrubs into dark blue carpenter jeans to ride the train back to Queens. But because she'd lingered so long with the Wests, Candice stayed on the floors into the evening and missed him.

She returned to the office feeling unusually defeated. The sputtering radiator that shouldn't even be on hissed at her as she began transcribing her notes from the day into Rabbi's antiquated computer system. The city was readying itself for the evening. Candice was just about to switch off the lights in the office when the dreaded '90s phone rang.

"Hello? Pastoral care."

The call was from six. Maternity.

"Oh shit. I mean, sorry, um, OK. Let me see if I can find the priest or the rabbi."

She hung up, then called both their cells, then texted. A few minutes went by. No answer. The scary '90s phone rang again.

"Did you find them? It's really urgent. The parents are hysterical," pressed the OBGYN nurse.

"I'm afraid not. Hang on, I'll be right down."

Rabbi was on his way home when she returned to the office from the sixth floor. He slid his elbows into his raincoat and shoved papers into a briefcase that wouldn't close.

"So, how did it go?"

She hadn't had time to center or prepare. She'd just gone down as quickly as possible, absentmindedly scrambling into the elevator, silently reciting the words of the baptism rite. Naturally, this had the effect of causing the people riding it to eye her stack of Bibles and chaplain's ID warily. Gloomily, the superstitious ones got off before their appointed floors.

Wrapped inside a blanket placed in a box, the stillborn body was long, still, and see-through as her aunt's glass eels. All that was missing was the ice for shipping. The dead baby looked peaceful, its transparent skin barely concealing its shrunken organs and tiny fingers like worms wrapped into little balls. *Together, they can assail any obstacle and get into any creek.* The parents, however, wailed like demons.

When his intern, lost in indiscernible emotion, did not answer, Rabbi pushed the elevator button and repeated his question more gently. "So, how did it go?"

"It was horrible, actually. I said the words right. I'm pretty sure about the ritual, but I don't think it did them any good. The parents, I mean. The way they wailed...it was so hard not to break down in front of them. Like, I know that's not the point. My feelings are not the point. But those tiny toes, even though they were not moving, they were still so beautiful ..."

Rabbi was in a rush. He'd baptized hundreds of dead Christian babies wrapped in blankets in boxes before. No big deal. They didn't make him cry anymore. Unlike Candice, he was a professional. Master of his emotions. Or was he?

"No, not that." He shook his head though something in his tone came loose. "I meant the Chinese family on 9 Uris."

"Oh, you mean the Wests? Yeah, it went alright. We connected some, but you know, no English."

Little Rocket Woman Ruins Ra

"RITTLE LOCKET IS FAVORITE with Washytown offy-shalls. She satisfy you no problem."

The madam, dressed conservatively in a gray suit, a purple scarf knotted at her neck, and three-inch heels, shoved her youngest and prettiest girl forward. In a slinky tube mini dress, platform shoes, and fake gold hoops, the girl's body-con existence seemed an affront to the madam's primness. Though her outfit screamed, the girl looked at Ra but said nothing. Plutonium pooled in her boiled-egg eyes as Ra paid the madam in American dollars.

In the filthy elevator, Ra's forearm brushed the girl's hip. She held her head high and shoulders back but lowered her head to look at him through ersatz eyelashes. He wheeled her around so that she could not see him.

"Stop that."

She tried to turn back around, making that same sulking face, balled up the end of his tie, and slid it into her mouth. He snatched the silk from between her teeth.

"Bitch, I said no. You stay behind. You don't get to see shit."

The girl crossed her arms and glared at the elevator doors with the wide stance of a perp in custody. As she tried not to look at him, her ribs flared against the tautness of her dress. Before the doors opened, he unfastened his gold Rolex ringed with diamonds, which Katya had given him for their first anniversary, and buried it in the secret pocket in the lining of his jacket.

The sheets were a kimchee color. A faint cabbage odor infused the room. Beyond the window, the motorway ribboning the otherwise off-grid oasis shook the drywall when tanker trucks freighting hazardous gases blew by. One every five or six minutes.

Little Rocket Woman slid out of her silvery tube dress and spread herself like the Sea of Japan on the bed. Her body was cylindrical, like a warhead, and her soft tofu skin glowed with a metallic sheen. Ra didn't bother unbuttoning his shirt or peeling off his socks. He pulled his arms out of his blazer, one by one, and laid it on the back of the chair by the door with the utmost care. Then, he shoved his tie into the girl's mouth and closed his incisors around her trigger points, biting until she bled. His fissile material unloaded quickly, the payload driving inward toward the negative space at the center of the girl's cavity.

Little Rocket Woman did not even pretend to detonate. She could tell which customers wanted her to fake rhapsody and which preferred simulated distress. She pegged Ra as a middleman of American bureaucracy. He needed to assert his simulacrum of power. The whole time, she remained kneeling on the bed with inner thighs of jelly emitting steam. Her face angled toward the rectangular window so that the yolks of her eyes lit up in the reflected headlights every time one of those terrifying steel tankards roared by.

As usual, it was over fairly quickly. His shirt stayed on the whole time, and his breathing barely sped up. Ra was more animated using his left hand to fight back into his trousers, than he had been fighting his way into her. Just looking at her now made him feel disgusted. With his right, he groped his phone and texted Katya: *Call the doc on Park and 81 and schedule full bloods for the week I'm back. PS Miss your tits.*

He reached next for the tie, patterned with tiny peregrine falcons. Its tip was notched with lipstick that did not come out when he rubbed it with his palm. For the first time, he wheeled around and faced the girl directly, pressing one hand with undue force on her mid-thigh. He shoved the fabric in Little Rocket Woman's face like one does a dog's nose in the piss puddled by the patio door.

"You see this? *Shay-shay* very fucking much. No tip for you. Ruined my favorite tie and didn't even pretend to come. Worst whore ever."

Little Rocket Woman pretended not to understand. She yanked her tube dress down over her crotch. Defiantly, it rolled back up her thighs. She stepped off the mattress, never breaking his gaze, then pushed her hips against his paunch. She pointed to her heart, then grabbed his scrotum.

"One six."

Her plutonium eyes bored into him while she cupped him gently, as he would have liked to be cupped when he was ramming her, but her arms weren't long enough to buttress herself against the mattress and caress him softly. Again and again, she repeated those two numbers.

"One six. One six."

"What the? Get off me, you crazy commie bitch!"

"Me. One six."

He hooked her by the elbow and flung her against the room. She crumpled into the corner, her body assuming the crescent moon shape of a fortune cookie. Hollow and curved, she arched against the filthy carpet, facing Ra directly and repeating the phrase like it was a slip of paper sealed inside her being. Some sort of fortune cookie curse.

The leather back seat of the sedan the embassy had dispatched for him was out-of-date but still passable as luxury. Ra extracted one of the best Cubans from his portable humidor. He ignored the commie driver with the deformed boxer's nose and slit eyes that diagonally dissected him in the rearview as he smoked idly out the window. He began to relax as the car turned its back on the periphery of Potonggang-guyok, the poorest of Pyongyang's nineteen districts, where the only attractions open to foreign visitors were the Victorious Liberation of the Fatherland Statue and the Potong River Pleasure Ground. They crossed the Simple Bridge, and he chucked his chewed-up cigar into the slate-colored slush. His hand automatically slid into his pocket but grazed nothing but air. His fucking blazer was gone.

Just then, a fire ignited in his crotch. A sudden engulfing combustion seared in the spaces between his cells. He dove his fingers into his pants and tried to soothe himself, but touching himself only made it turn orange and swell. Few things made Ra panic, and the thought of contracting Fournier's gangrene was one of them. Once, on an assignment in an undisclosed desert location, Ra and his men had stormed a goatherder's hut and discovered an insurgent naked from the waist down. The man was writhing next to his Kalashnikov on the baked mud floor. Instead of shooting him on site, the American medics (who were all men), horrified by the rare disease, put aside geopolitics and treated the man's universality surgically.

For two hours, the commie urged the sedan on, and the gnawing in Ra's pants worsened. He dialed the madam from his secure line, but she did not pick up.

"I hope Trump wipes this shithole off the map."

"Yes, sir. We go off map very soon," the diver said, smiling a plastic smile.

They rolled along the highway behind the tankers, which were so frequent now that they formed a continuous fleet. The fat face of the boy dictator smiled down on the lanes like a maniac pug on every billboard. Those squinty eyes were everywhere, even pasted onto a poster behind the bed in the Pleasure Garden. As he had been unloading into Little Rocket Woman, he'd not known where to look—at the dictator or the girl.

The sedan jerked north and entered the mountainous terrain of Kilju County. As they climbed, the mountain collapsed into a smattering of army-green scrub, skeleton forests, desiccated lakes, nothing, just rock. They drove against the dawn, and the road beneath them seemed to tremble slightly. Two more hours and forty-seven minutes later, they reached their destination.

Three visible tunnel entrances. Security waved Ra through and granted him access underground via the westernmost one. For the next nine hours, he supervised what he'd been sent there to do, which the UN's policymakers insisted had to be done: the health examination, psychological interview, and nutrition survey. The participants snaked into lines, signed informed consent paperwork, stripped off their hazmat coveralls, then stuck out their purple tongues. At the same time, the medics numbered the protons swimming beneath their eyelids and around their ribs. The workers' bodies were as withered as the trees shivering at Mount Mantap's midsection. Their eyes, windows to their vital organs, were lifeless holes incapable of cancer or despair. The pharmaceutical subcontractors jotted down more than once: *significant, irreversible damage*. And Ra? He just stood there, looking intimidating, while the friction in his balls intensified. Intravenous flames ricocheted through his cellular labyrinth. It was like someone had swabbed the inside of his testes with hydrochloric acid, lowered them into the centrifuge, and hit spin.

People who had been to Punggye-ri were not allowed to return to Pyongyang. When it was done, one of the People's captains escorted Ra back out of the tunnel and thanked him. Before he climbed onto the chopper, he stared one last time into the angry eyes of the nearest commie, itched his scrotum, then spat on the hollow, contaminated ground.

Though the blood appointment had been made, Katya was not in the apartment when Ra deplaned from Seoul via West Virginia. Often, like a calico displaying its displeasure at its owner's absence by clawing the leather couch and then pissing in the newly torn grooves, the missus skulked away on short-haul trips to avoid crisscrossing her husband, inbound from international professional exploits. It was almost summer, so Ra figured she'd jumped the Jitney to Montauk with the SoulCycle girls.

The next day, trying hard not to scratch, he made his report to the UN, then cabbed off to the white coats at Weil-Cornell. He was in disbelief when he was cleared. Like all patients in pain, he reiterated his symptoms with greater severity when the young doctor disregarded his concerns.

"Only women display atypical symptoms like fatigue, increased appetite, and uncontrolled crying," insisted the good-looking MD with a wink. "Don't worry about it, dude. Everything is fine."

Ra returned to the office on Monday, itchy and uncomfortable, although no one could tell anything was wrong. Nobody knew any of Ra's secrets. Not lawyers, not doctors, not bosses, not women. They all guessed: Where is he really from (Iran? Israel?), what language does he really speak (Farsi? Yiddish?), what is his actual job title (private agent? government goon)? Only Ra's bagel man knew anything about his truest self. Georgy at the Pick-A-Bagel on Lexington was his countryman. The first time Ra went to that Pick-A-Bagel, he gave the bagel man the pseudonym "Rayman" to call out when his order was ready. And the bagel man, wittily, had truncated the false name to "Ra."

"You know, man, because your fancy watch is beautiful and shines like the ancient sun god. Scallion or regular cream cheese today?"

When Ra came back from the DPRK with jet-lagged eyes and horror on his breath, his colleagues ignored the slight stiffness in the walk and the suit trousers ballooning at the crotch. They slapped him on the back, tossed cigars his way, and congratulated him on another "gig well done." Everyone that is, except Kevin.

Kevin was the colleague Ra hated most because he was a young, handsome Hong Kong-born, British-educated ex-intelligence official with long limbs like a prince who always wore a beat-up Barbour jacket to signify his laissez-faire approach to privilege and intellectualism. Kevin was out of the office when Ra first returned from Pyongyang, but when he finally reappeared, sporting a brand-new gold Rolex and looking tanned but nervous, he was suddenly staring at Ra all the time.

"Do I have shit on my face or something, Kevin?"

"No! It's nothing. It's just … well, you look a little rough, man. How was it over there in the DPRK?"

"Not as rough as where you've been, apparently. Have a nice holiday?"

"Sort of. I just bought a house in East Hampton. I've been waiting a while to make a move. Just waiting for the right girl, you know?"

Two more weeks passed, and Katya did not come home. The fission in Ra's scrotum intensified, so he went back to the doctor, who told him again that his blood was "cool" and not to worry. Every morning, he went downstairs around the corner and across Lexington Avenue to Pick-a-Bagel. It was the only part of his day that was safe and sane. Georgy grinned at him like a real friend as he scooped out moguls of scallion cream cheese.

"Everything for Monsieur Ra, and salt for Madame Ra."

Georgy was an honest man who came from where Ra came from and shared his values. Even so, Ra could not admit to the cream-cheese scooper that his wife was someplace unknown, stonewalling him. That would almost be like telling his father back home that he was a murderer and an adulterer. Where they were from, old-world values still threaded society together, keeping the kingdom from blowing itself to smithereens. Even though it humiliated Ra, he thanked Georgy playfully, paid for Katya's bagel, and carried two coffees home.

When Ra returned to his building, the expression on the doorman's face told him everything he needed to know.

"Mr. Ra, sir. Please, I need you to remain calm. The gentleman said he was your friend, a colleau—"

But Ra's training was autonomous. The doorman's aorta was throbbing beneath his thumb before the Styrofoam cups brimming with half-and-half went off like bombs on the lobby floor. He didn't have to kick the door down because all six bolts were still unbolted. He saw the beat-up Barbour slung haphazardly over an imitation "Louis Kanz" chair (as Katya was so fond of calling it) in the entryway before the barbarian to whom it belonged.

One year later, Ra was not in terrible pain, emotional distress, or any especially hideous discomfort. His balls still blazed, but with the help of a geriatric chink on Baxter Street who gave him festering kelp to boil, most days, he endured it with the dignity of Joan of Arc.

Ra's divorce was finalized shortly after the establishment of the forever presidency. Before the rioting ended, he visited a psychic on West 17th Street. He paid her twenty bucks, then immediately regretted it. He hated how the fat gypsy peered at him over her crystal ball and minor Egyptian deities (Nile God Hapy, Harpocrates, Harendotes, etc.) made of painted plastic—and whispered like the place was bugged.

"Your doctor is not lying. There is nothing physically wrong with you. Their science will never find it. Only your spiritual ailment is real, but it should not diminish your quality of life. It ought to compound it with a kind of celestial 'electricity.' It is your destiny to purify yourself and this world like your people's priests of old."

Safe in the anonymity of Sixth Avenue, Ra brushed off the bodega prophecy like the useless words about warriors and sages that a Jungian in Crown Heights had thrown at him after the divorce. *Psychosomatic* was the word professionals kept agreeing on to describe the excruciating sensation that his penis was slowly rotting from the inside out. According to their expert assessments, neither his age group, income quartile, nor employment status could sufficiently account for what they otherwise were convinced were warning signs of "suicidal ideation." But they had not done what he had done to protect his clients' subcontractors toiling away under that radioactive mountain on the other side of the world. They had not fucked Little Rocket Woman looking the pug dictator in the slanty eyes or lost their wives to *Kevin*. What did they know about killing—oneself or others?

After that trip to DPRK, the company stopped sending Ra on exotic assignments. Most of his work was banality now. He leaned on his standing desk and pushed digital files around. Kevin, meanwhile, had married Katya and turned freelance consultant. From time to time, the firm would hire him on a project basis. One afternoon, Mr. Katya stepped off the elevator looking more handsome than ever for a meeting to which Ra was not invited. The colleagues saluted him like a returning war hero. The democracy! The nobility! If only they'd seen their prince that morning when Ra had come home with a bag of bagels to find Kevin helping Katya stuff all her belongings into boxes. He had tried to smash Kevin's nose so that it looked like the commie driver in the DPRK, but the younger man was quicker and stronger. He had disarmed Ra by pinning his check to the surface of the hallway credenza. The leg of Katya's beloved Louis Kanz chair had snapped in the scrum.

"That's why I'm leaving you!" Ra's woman had screamed, kicking the broken chair and dragging the fleet of Goyards, which Ra had purchased and had monogrammed, to the open door.

"Because you've found a gook dick to suck on?"

"Because you're a hateful, violent brute!"

"At least I'm not a dumb brainless whore!"

With Kevin still holding him down, Katya spat on the back of his neck.

"I hope your dick withers and falls off into the belly of your next third world child sex slave."

Ra still lived in the same building. Only now, he lived in the penthouse. He'd sworn off women, boiled antifungal Chinese herbs daily, and joined seven cigar clubs. Smokers & Jokers on Columbus was his latest. The first time he went there, he stayed all night. At 3:16 a.m., a young Asian woman, clearly intoxicated, lurched at him.

"Get off me, slut!" he'd shouted and shoved her so that she crashed to the floor. When she lifted her chin, blood dripped from her teeth.

"You bastard!"

The drunk woman had flung herself at Ra and tried to scratch him. She reminded him of Little Rocket Woman, what she might look like now if the madam had allowed her to live this long. Ra subdued the hysteria with one deft motion before the bar's security could rush to his aid. Together, they'd bottled the drunk Asian out of the bar and into a cab. She went cursing and threatening to go to the police. The manager anointed him a hero.

"Come back anytime, Ra. Here, you will always smoke and drink for free."

The next night, Ra was back on the same stool, puffing Cubans and sipping twenty-five-year-old McCallan on the house. Shortly before midnight, a young couple carrying Playbills slipped onto the stools beside him. The man wore a clipped beard and had bright teal eyes. He helped his date out of her coat, and the fabric caught on her elbow. A first, maybe second, date. Ra listened to their conversation—occupational hazard. They talked intelligently about art and religion. He learned that the guy was a Jew, and the girl was a Buddhist; he was a painter, and she was an art history professor; they had recently met at some sort of gallery thing.

Ra wistfully eavesdropped, thinking how nice it must be to be young, educated White Americans like them. This was why tawny-skinned dual-citizens like him did what they did: to make way for a world where these two could meet on the job, flirt, fall in love, and one day, die or get divorced. Deliberately, Ra blew his smoke their way.

"Oh, I'm sorry. Does it bother you? Because I can turn away …"

"No, it's OK," replied the woman. She was wearing a red sweater, the color of the bar's walls. She had a friendly face, pretty but unpretentious. "We don't mind."

"Can I offer you one? Do you smoke?"

"Only cigarettes," replied the young man.

"So not the same thing," added the girl teasingly.

This amused Ra, so he paid for their drinks. He even offered to buy them food, but they refused. Even though they sensed his loneliness, they wanted to be left alone. They thanked him, but he continued to engage.

"I understand. May this be a blessed night that you remember always, and may you propagate the earth with your prosperity."

They knew there was no escaping Ra, who lit his fourth cigar.

"Maybe we should go," the young man whispered (which suited his designs anyhow).

She touched her hand to her date's. Ra stared at them without realizing his jealousy. Suddenly, Ra was cognizant of his scrotum. The infernal itching—it was gone. He touched the young woman on the arm, just above the elbow. She shuddered, and he shook off the sudden urge to follow her home.

"Wait, young friends. I have one last question before you go."

The young man stepped intuitively between them, but the girl gently pushed him aside so that she came close to Ra.

"Sure," she said. "Shoot."

"In your expert opinion, what's the one work of art in New York City that everyone should see at least once, if not more, during their time here? The heart, if you will, of our city's art?"

The man clung to the woman and started to say something erudite about MoMA, but she shook free of his grip.

"That's easy," she interrupted. "Dendur."

Ra didn't know what "Dendur" was, so he looked it up the moment they left the bar. What he read captivated him until closing. In the 1960s, the Egyptian government started building the dam at Aswan, which swelled the ancient river goddess with rage. Lady Nile's diverted tears would have drowned so many famous sites, but the UN swooped in, hawkish to tear apart ancient Egypt brick by brick and ship her off to the West for safekeeping. The Temple of Dendur, completed under the orders of Rome's first emperor to honor the exotic goddess Isis in 10 BCE, was taken apart in the 1970s, then put back together, cartouche by cartouche (most of which simply read "Pharaoh"), in a trapezoidal glass box overlooking Central Park in the middle of Manhattan.

Ra surveilled the Sackler Wing for six days, just like any other job. He sat there all Sunday afternoon and into the evening until the museum closed. On Monday, he went again. The sun shone through the glass windows like it was shining on the desert. A mother and daughter from the Midwest howled with laughter as they "walked like an Egyptian" for the father's hungry phone camera. The child trotted around the temple, and the soles of her sneakers lit up.

On Tuesday, it was gray, and Ra learned from a disgruntled security guard (who did not believe that his overtime pay was being reasonably calculated) that, on Saturday night, UNICEF would be holding a fundraiser gala for their charity: END SEX TRAFFICKING NOW. To Ra's surprise, while the guard had noticed him, he deemed Ra's presence wholly benevolent.

"You come here a lot, brother. You an Egyptologist or something?"

"Yes, brother. Something like that."

On Wednesday, rain. A man with shoulder-length silvered hair dressed all in black sat with one arm heavy on his knee, the other on his thigh, and a laptop bag against his hip. His nose was pharaonic. Only he, Ra suspected in retrospect when reviewing his final notes, might have suspected what Ra was up to. Thursday, more rain. Schoolchildren in pretty blue pinafores ran around holding hands in rows of two. Their screams of delight scratched the ceiling. Friday, sunshine. A pair of lovers, illicit, Ra knew from years of doing what he had done, striding slowly with their eyes down and their fingers wandering, thrilling at their secret openness.

Kevin came into the office that week to work on another project from which Ra was excluded. The men were omniscient when it came to each other. Perhaps, it was the result of swimming in the waters of the same woman. Maybe, it was just the nature of the Hamptons crowd. Finally, on Friday, Kevin followed Ra into the men's room and confronted him at the urinal.

"That doesn't look so good, dude. Have you had that checked out?"

"Of course, I've had it checked out, douche. I get it checked out by the hottest bitches every night, you wouldn't believe," he barked, then whisked his dick away.

Finally, Saturday came. Cloudless and clean.

As usual, Ra put on his best suit and drove two blocks to double park outside the cream cheese assembly line at Pick-A-Bagel. Georgy was up to his elbows in a mound of low-fat scallion cream. When he saw Ra, he grinned.

"Morning, boss. Everythings and salts with lox and scallion cream cheese?"

"You know it, brother." They rubbed hairy knuckles.

Ra paid and took his coffee into the car. Even though Pick-A-Bagel was only eight blocks away, he drove to the Met. The security guard was used to him now, so they exchanged friendly smiles. Around noon, PR people dressed in black filed into the space. They yelled at the caterers throwing white tablecloths over round banquet tables. At two, carts of crystal and napkins were pushed in. At four, servers and interns arrived.

The security guard ambushed Ra just before five.

"I'm sorry, friend. I know you usually like to stay until closing, but I must ask you to leave now. They need to finish setting up for the event."

He dismissed Ra toward the American Wing with a wave. Ra wandered through the American Wing to the Assyrian and Near Eastern section until the museum, open until nine on weekends, finally closed. Just before nine, he went into a men's room on the balcony floor, changed into the tuxedo he'd brought in a small messenger bag, then scrunched up his Italian suit and the bag into the trash. He strolled right past the event security guarding the museum's north flank. In the Sackler Wing, a celebrity philanthropist breathed into a microphone between courses.

"Ladies and gentlemen, we are here tonight because more than ten million women are subjected to modern slavery globally ..."

A smattering of soft applause. Unable to force himself to mingle, Ra exited the space, nodding at the guards, and disappeared into Grace Rainey Rogers Auditorium. He sat in the darkness before the empty stage, feeling like he was rehearsing for something.

For almost four hours, he waited.

After midnight, the museum was silent as a tomb. Ra crept out of the auditorium and wove along with the shadows of the sarcophagi toward the Sackler Wing. The tables had all been stripped. Beyond the slanted glass panels, a handful of satellites masqueraded as stars. He crossed the moat, stepping lightly over the second-century bronze crabs hijacked from Alexandria with the solemnity of ancient worshippers. He approached the temple and caressed the images of papyrus and lily plants carved into the temple's base. He kissed his palms one by one, then touched them to the two columns on the porch. Finally, he entered the main temple.

Isis's headless priestess, who did not belong there, was waiting for him. With her right shin, the frozen stone was stepping toward him. The weight of the destruction of worlds was braided into her granite hair and smeared on her lips. In her fist, she clenched the wand of Upper and Lower Egypt.

He could not bear the melancholia any longer. At last, Ra's diverted tears flooded. He fell to his knees. Cartilage contacting the stone made a sound that tried to fill the space, then faded away. The necrosis in his nether regions flared up with a pain he'd never known. It was as if the goddess had received the offering of his tears and responded by kneeing him in the balls. His entire form seemed to collapse inward on the point of that pain. All-consuming, never-ending, eternal. It was the pain of annihilation. A pump on a timer turned on, and the moat encircling the temple's dais gurgled. Ra kissed the arch of the statue's extended foot.

"Little Rocket Woman, forgive me!"

Above the faces carved in limestone over the facade of the museum's entrance nested a sky god who had taken the shape of a falcon. He scowled at the veterans selling hot dogs; they refused to give up their prime Fifth Avenue spots and slept in lawn chairs squeezed inside their carts. They watched television on their phones. Television! At a museum! The David Koch fountains pooled in the streetlight, smooth as millponds. A few cockroaches scuttled along the museum steps, hunting in the early light of first dawn. Ra was attracted to the glow flicking around their backs and felt his talons stir in response to yawning in his belly, but no.

I'm going to wait. For another eternity, if that's what it takes.

It took another six years.

At last, when they did come, they came with a child—a boy with Kevin's puppy face studded with Katya's hazel eyes. Either parent grasped one puffy little hand. The Trump-era tax cuts had been kind to them. Kevin looked richer than ever, and Katya had brand-new breasts to offset the years' droops in her cheeks. The boy was dressed in a miniature version of his father's decomposing Barbour, and the mother had one on too. The young family marched up the museum steps holding hands.

"Are you excited to see the temple? They brought it here all the way from Egypt, stone by stone ..."

The mother's Russian accent was much smoother now. The boy bounced eagerly. Last summer, they visited Europe, only lately populist and safe for New Regimers like themselves, since the tide had turned at the end of the last war. But Egypt, the boys' dearest interest, still remained unsafe for travelers like them, citizens of a semi-presidential government.

Those who claimed to have seen what happened next said it happened so fast that they could not say for sure what they saw.

"A hawk," the Chinese tour group told the NYPD.

"An eagle," said veterans selling hot dogs to the *Post*.

"It wasn't either of those things," insisted Georgy to his wife when he came home that evening and found her glued to MAGA News Corps' prime time.

After the declaration of the forever presidency, the cops lost control of the looting. Georgy had been among the Brown and Black men scooped up, smeared, and popped into prison for racketeering. Four years later, when he came out, it was a different nation, and Pick-a-Bagel on Lexington, which had been run by Ashkenazi Jews from Flatbush, was closed. Now, as part of his state-sanctioned parole, he worked as a trash-picker-upper for the City of New York, which was why he happened to be emptying a forest green garbage can on Fifth Avenue and 82nd when the birdlike creature swooped down from the roof of the museum and ripped out the little rich boy's throat.

In the chaos that ensued, nobody had noticed the convicted criminal plucking a diamond-encrusted gold Rolex, which had simply rained out of the sky during the shower of blood, out of the garbage can. But Georgy knew that watch. He recognized the bird. Even if he'd had all his legal rights revoked, he was still a man who never forgot his brothers.

"So, what was it then?" demanded Mrs. Georgy, not knowing what her husband had found and what he was planning to do with his find—namely, hawk it, use it to purchase illegal documentation, return to his ancestral homeland, then marry a much younger, attractive village girl.

Georgy thought fondly back to his scallion scooping days and grinned. He'd known about the two bagels and the two coffees and what would happen to the US government all along.

"It was the end of the world, my dear, in the shape of the falcon."

Happy Ending

AT 9 AM, MRS. ZIMMERMAN began the process. First, she sliced her aching skeleton gingerly from its cocoon of cornflower-colored French linen sheets. Something was *very* wrong with her left ankle again. The swollen ball joint gleamed at her, the color of an iris bouquet. Contrary to what Stephen muttered before turning away from her in bed, she had *not* slept off the twist. She padded barefoot away from the bedroom with uneven, deliberate care. She refused to wince past the library to arrive at the kitchen where secretions from last night's altercation with Stephen lingered innocuously as leftovers. With her therapist off in the Azores, she could do without retraumatizing before noon.

"We'll talk when I get home this evening," the husband had muttered when he extracted himself from the far side of their bed. But it wasn't a question, and he wasn't looking at her when he said it. "Five o'clock, we'll have a cocktail, as usual for a Thursday. What do you say, dear?"

A grapefruit was brought to her. She was 99% sure that the docile girl Mrs. Zimmerman called Chloe, who fetched it, was Vietnamese (Mrs. Zimmerman always asked about origins in interviews because women like her could no longer afford to appear out of touch). She nibbled the oversized organic fruit without sugar and asked for one piece of burnt bacon. Unlike her husband, she had no qualms about not keeping kosher now that the kids were grown and gone. With traces of charred pork still on her tongue, she dressed and then drifted into the sun-drenched breakfast room with Tuscan yellow walls. There, she set about returning the much younger wives' morning-after thank-you text messages. They all thought last night's dinner was *ah-mazing*. Their uxorial perfunctoriness had impressed Mrs. Zimmerman, but she'd judged the girls as vapid millennials who didn't understand a thing about husbands or real feminism.

She hunched at the little mid-century writing desk, basking in the beauty of her penmanship. Handwritten notes with embossed envelopes were incomparably more civilized than replying to vulgar texts. It was up to her to set an example for the next generation or what would become of Park Avenue?

An hour or so passed. She dressed again, this time for lunch. She avoided looking at her heavy crocodile wallet and decided to leave it behind. She extracted some cash and concealed the rest in a dresser drawer.

Then, the doorman rang up.

"Your car, ma'am."

Mrs. Zimmerman hobbled to the elevator, ostrich kitten heels in hand. She pushed the button, then slid the slingbacks over her chapped heels. Right away, the left ankle seized. She forced the foot in regardless, causing an unseemly wince to escape her matte peach-glossed lips. Into the fin-de-siècle birdcage she loped, and Joe (the attractive young elevator attendant, whom she was pretty sure was Puerto Rican and called *Jose*) did her the courtesy of making deferential eye contact, offering a polite "afternoon, ma'am," and leaving it at that. The bronze youth flipped the antique lever. The carriage shuddered as the ornate wrought-iron gates clamped shut and jerked into what Mrs. Zimmerman considered a pleasant rush of vertigo.

The driver, Muzzammil, was waiting for his mistress on the ground floor. Standing tall, he was attractive, which increased her pleasant feelings when she looked at him. The chauffeur had come to her with an impossible foreign name, so she'd been forced to anglicize it to *Max*. Unlike Arturo, her husband's longtime driver, accomplice, and nemesis on staff, Max was *her* hire, her man. He worked for the Missus for a reason. Two months back, Mrs. Zimmerman had dismissed Arturo without her husband's permission and replaced him with Max. They'd never discussed her overreach. There'd been no fight. And yet, the incident loomed more prominent in their decades-long marriage than any of Thomas' extramarital affairs. The staffing switch-up was as far as Mrs. Zimmerman had ever dared to go in wielding her will over her husband's.

Max, meanwhile, didn't mind being patronized by his patroness. He relished his status as an adored/reviled, ethically ambiguous changeling. Where employment in NYC was concerned, things could be infinitely worse. He could be working at an Amazon fulfillment center in Secaucus, as a Lyft driver, or not working at all. Mrs. Z was not creepy toward him. Instead, she was kind and doting in a nice, white auntie sort of way. Max hadn't seen his biological aunties in four years—they lived on the other side of the world with his mother and very sketchy internet—so he soaked up the attention like sun rays carefully captured and DHL'd to his shared Bronx apartment.

Mrs. Zimmerman slid across the marbled lobby, anticipating the warmth of Max's friendly young face.

But when he saw her trying to hide her hobble, the chauffeur frowned and said, "Are you alright, ma'am? Something's wrong with your foot again. Here, let me help you."

He pointed. The finger was dark, dry, and hairy. It repulsed her like the desiccated $8 hot dogs abandoned by tourists and cockroaches on the Metropolitan Museum of Art steps. However, she didn't despise him for his coarseness.

"I'm alright, Max, really. I just twisted my ankle at Pilates yesterday."

Mrs. Zimmerman knew that Max knew he had driven her to no such appointment. Pilates had been scrapped months ago. Barre class was the thing now. Her hobbling was not new, just worse.

Four chrome finish wheels turned down Park Avenue. Soon, the distinguished title would dissolve into nameless asphalt, crisscrossed with rats, garbage, and far too many trendy sneakers. Though she kept a strict practice of never saying so unless surrounded by her girls beneath Sarabeth's cobalt awnings, it made perfect sense that numbers replaced names in the most chaotic parts of the city. It was imperative to impress at least a vague sense of *order*. But then again, most imperatives do make sense to mothers of three and wives of husbands like Stephen G. Zimmerman, senior named partner at Byrne, Zimmerman, and Smith LLP.

The black car barreled down the Bowery, heading straight for Chinatown. That ruddy shadow beneath the Brooklyn Bridge was as foreign to Mrs.

Zimmerman as Beijing. She'd been there, naturally, but hadn't found it overly appealing. It was a spiritless city of businesses and brothels where people sold their souls for stock shares and skylines as deregulated as the markets that built them. China's skyscrapers were starting to swallow Manhattan's infrastructure, sending the city's architecture (and maybe one day Wall Street itself!) into obscurity's grave like an unwanted daughter. Therefore, to hail the Chinese as the future was not only treacherous but adjacent to kowtowing to Communist tyranny. Besides, her eldest, Aaron, had just shipped off to Shanghai for a summer internship at HSBC. That's why, at present, all of Asia for her resembled a young onion-skinned prostitute trying to steal her beloved white knight away.

An elderly Asian woman wearing a bleached denim vest over a floral-printed cotton dress appeared beyond the car window. Mrs. Zimmerman assumed this was Canal Street (it wasn't, it was Baxter). Thin, slightly bowed, and snow-haired, the woman struggled to pull her plastic roller grocery cart across the crooked stoop toward an unrestored tenement walk-up. Above the door glowed a neon sign: *Heavenly Hands: Qi Gong Tui Na, Chinese Massage.*

Mrs. Zimmerman wondered whether the crone was old enough to have been produced by a generation in which feet were bound. These things about other cultures interested her; atavistic barbarism later expunged by contact with civilization was charming to behold. The pleasure of association was the same one got through luxury travel to third-world countries or private tours of natural history museums.

The intimate dinner thrown the evening prior had been capped at twelve, and she'd worn the cream Carolina Herrera dress she'd been saving all season. As usual, the culinary presentation was impeccable, but when it was over, Stephen, with gin on his teeth and his black bow tie loosened at the Adam's Apple, had told his wife to summon Arturo. Even though she hadn't known precisely where he was going, she always knew where he was when he was not where he was supposed to be: "downtown."

Since the 50s, "downtown" has served as an uptown catchphrase for all manner of sin, like gay men giving each other blowjobs and crack dens filled with runaways from the antisemitic Midwest. In any case, all Mrs. Zimmerman remembered was not saying anything, except maybe something about hailing a taxi and then lots of shouting. She remembered Stephen's black crocodile wallet. Bloated with too many bills and receipts, it protruded from his fist. She also remembered bone meeting marble, followed by the brutal slam of the front door.

Gently, Mrs. Zimmerman put a hand on her ankle. The ache, misalignment, and throb raced right up her calf, through her knee socket, along the sides of her hips, and into her lower back. The ankle was its emanation point, but when she bothered to direct her awareness there, how the pain radiated! She personified her kitten heels and sued them mentally for irreparable harm.

Though she was never hungry, it was always too late to cancel. Why would she want to anyway? It wasn't like they were walking anywhere. Besides, lunch with the girls was the only thing that could cheer her up when she was in this mood. At least when the four of them put their Black Cards together, their Botoxed cheeks permanently frozen in the grimace of pleasantry, worldviews aligned, and things were almost OK.

Out of courtesy, Max always announced their arrival three blocks before: "Nearly there, Ma'am," he whistled, and three blocks later, they were on the corner of Bayard and Mulberry.

"Thank you, Max. I suppose we shouldn't be more than two hours, so get me at three. Stephen returns at five today, and I must be home in plenty of time."

"Yes, Ma'am." Max leaped out of the vehicle to yank open the passenger door. "Enjoy your lunch."

Mrs. Zimmerman emerged with the gravity of politicians arriving at Parliament to be photographed. She felt assured that Max made her look good (people were staring). She gazed around at all the squiggly pictograms and skinned ducks hanging by their necks in the restaurant windows, feeling like a foreigner in her own city. There was something of a thrill about the unexpected exotic. Still, she quickly dismissed it as ridiculous, clasped her small lizard clutch (which gave her a sense of security although it only held her keys, phone, and a fistful of cash), and swished toward the door. Humidity slammed into her like a brick wall. Where bone met bone inside the ankle joint ground against her kitten heel, forcing her to shift her weight irregularly from foot to foot. She paused to compose herself and ran a see-through hand through her freshly touched-up blowout. Lastly, she smoothed away the pain in her cheeks before nodding Max off and entering the restaurant.

Mrs. Zimmerman swiped off her oversized sunglasses, feeling reticent. Some uncomfortable emotion froze in her eyes. Unfortunately, she could do nothing about that. All her ladies were already there. She took the last empty seat at the much-coveted window table in the newly Michelin-starred Shanghai Parlor.

"Sorry, I'm late, girls. I was recuperating from last night's disaster."

"Disaster?" echoed the chorus. "Again?"

"Stephen caught me fucking the handsome brown chauffeur again."

Did she just say that? Oops. She had. They all knew it was perfectly untrue, both the admission of adultery and casually intended racism, but they did not know what to say back. The words hung there, ignored until Mrs. Zimmerman struck them from the record.

"Oh, I'm just kidding, ladies! You know, just the usual bungle with the caterers. Kids in this city can't do anything right these days. They all think they're stars."

"Ugh, *caterers*," sighed the relieved women in unison.

And just like that, lunch began. No mere meal, the affair was a highly sophisticated and synchronistic ritual complete with minute yet exacting demands of menu alteration, sommelier Olympics, and a choreographed sampling of each others' plates, course after course. Between mouthfuls of Peking duck with Royal Beluga Caviar and crispy stir-fry venison washed down with gulps of Chardonnay, the women took turns vacillating between griping about the open disobedience of their college-aged children and pre-menopausal wailing. Mrs. Zimmerman's sullenness, despite her best efforts, was not lost on her friends. The other three women astutely avoided their other favorite topics—dry beds, absent husbands, and younger, blonder secretaries—like a progressive at a hedge fund to-do.

The dessert menu took nearly three hours to be brought and haggled over. The food filibusters continued through consumption as the quartet performed their dietary sins. When the last drop of fat-attacking oolong had been drunk, beneath the diamond-encrusted face of Mrs. Zimmerman's Cartier watch, she could see it was coming up on three. She politely hastened her associates toward the bill.

Typically, the ladies had a penchant for lingering, preferring to wallow in the misery of loving company just a bit longer before returning uptown to do more of the same, either with their therapists or alone in their respective palatial abodes. But today, something was not quite right with Mrs. Zimmerman. Typically, their friend was a reservoir of interior design wisdom, but she hardly chimed in when the topic of

Meryl's new color palette came up. All lunch long, she sighed. She sighed continuously throughout the summit of the absent children, the diatribe on the new fall collections, the renovation wreaking havoc in the basement at Barneys, and the reorganizing of late summer clam bakes. Other women can smell humiliation as clearly as a freshly uncapped bottle of Chanel No. 5, which is precisely what happened.

At last, Karen waved her wrist weakly, indicating a passive desire for the check. Mrs. Zimmerman couldn't help but let a "thank god" escape her lips. It was quiet but audible, immediately after which the menopausal table slumped into an awkwardly pregnant silence. It was as if they all knew someone should ask their friend that all-important question, "Are you OK?"

They all already knew she wasn't. If they asked, they'd be sorry at the reams of memoir that tumbled out by way of an answer. No matter how many self-help books had passed between their French-manicured hands, they were not therapists. They *hated* listening to each other's miserable lives! Worse still was the resonance that crept into the arduously maintained tummy, followed soon after by powerlessness, self-loathing, and hatred of said tummy for holding onto baked goods and painful emotions. Ostensibly, they cared. But no one dared put their consideration into action.

Three Amexes clumped together and overlapped slightly on the white tablecloth. The women, her friends, were mute now, but Mrs. Zimmerman knew that would not be the case later. Now, they were incapable when she needed them to look into her blue eyes, hear her words, and *not* give advice. It was like taking them to a farm in a non-ironic way and without any phones or cameras. But later, when she was gone, over yet another round of tea, she knew her friends would fill the negative space vacated by her Park Avenue Princess body with a scarecrow of hearsay and gossip. Then, when they were good and drunk, they'd set her effigy on fire. Like his teacher Plato, Aristotle (who knew nothing of neurons) saw pain not as a physical sensation but as pathos, the soul's passions. Here, the heart, not the brain, was implicated as the central sensing organ. On this and a few other essential points, Mrs. Zimmerman and the Socratics agreed.

Mrs. Zimmerman pulled her new lizard skin clutch with the skull clasp from her lap. Her friends were relieved to see this season's must-have, sold-out, super-waitlisted accessory before their very eyes. They anchored themselves in it and channeled their supportive impulses into complimenting the cuteness of the bag. For them, distraction was kindness. Mrs. Zimmerman wanted to rip off the skull clasp and shove it in Karen's eye socket before jamming the box clutch down Meryl's throat. Instead, she smiled, blushed, and thanked them profusely.

To expedite the interminable exiting process, Mrs. Zimmerman overpaid in cash—nearly all she had in her wallet. She did not ask for change. Wincing, she levitated on kitten heels while all four women stepped merrily behind her onto the congested sidewalk. Whenever they "stepped out" anywhere as a carefully styled cohort, they felt like they were sixteen and coming out of the cafeteria into the sunshine to make lesser mortals feel bad about themselves all over again. But the corner of Bayard and Mulberry was hardly the quad at Choate, and the twin unpleasantries of immigrants and tourists immediately assailed the four White women.

Like sunflowers, their faces intuitively sought a photogenic background and the best light. They pointed themselves naturally toward Pell Street, so narrow yet colorful. Compact storefronts with awnings covered in Chinese scrawls made the ladies feel as though they were in China, even though when they did visit such places, they only went to places that reminded them of places they already knew, like famous luxury spas and Louis Vuitton flagship stores. At home or abroad, this ruled out close encounters with undesirable entities like fruit carts, first-generation and second-generation immigrants, busloads of Chinese tourists, a pound of broccoli for 69 cents, plastic Buddha statues, and all manner of cooking equipment pressed against the upper window of a two-story emporium, Thai grocers, Vietnamese grocers, Indonesian grocers, Filipino grocers, fish with their bellies up and glassy eyes displayed on trays lined with ice, "designer" bags laid out on garbage bags at the sandaled feet of African men, people dressed in loose-fitting yellow garments making obscure hand signals in front of a sign that says "FALUN DAFA IS GOOD," foot spas with neon signs that lead upstairs where free Chinese whisky shots await, knick-knack purveyors, foreign (non-Swiss) banks, dim sum entrepreneurs, and bubble tea shops. The noise, the smell, the crowd, so many foreign signs they could not read! Even though they could see the Manhattan Bridge Gate, they would tell everyone back uptown that it had practically been Flushing and totally stressed them out. It did not help that the September sun also renewed its force in the afternoon, deliberately intending to abuse them.

All four uptown ladies emitted a sweaty glow during the short trot from restaurant to curb (no more than half a city block). Mrs. Zimmerman air-kissed each on either cheek, trying not to brush against any sticky makeup. She stood there waving and smiling fakely until her friends twisted away toward Meryl's husband's enormous Escalade, which promptly swallowed them up. Mrs. Zimmerman thought for a moment of Jonah and the whale, then of Rabbi Silverman (whom she hadn't seen since going to college; he was probably dead), then pulled out her phone.

Ten past three, it told her, *and you're at 10% battery*. Mrs. Zimmerman dialed Max. Straight to voicemail. She dialed again. Voicemail again.

Where was he? Did he expect her to take a taxi home or risk her life on the subway? A mere seventeen dollars in change was left in a sleeve pocket in the silk lining of the $8,000 purse. Not enough for a cab home. She cursed her husband for polluting her feelings about wallets. Like all misfortunes that befell her, this was *his* fault.

She dialed Max a third time when her phone abruptly excused itself from consciousness. *So, 10% isn't a warning. It's the last call.* She put a vicious hex on all of Silicon Valley while silently calculating the percentage created by dividing her current age by her ideal lifespan. After doing the math, she decided to wait.

Mrs. Zimmerman stood baking on the corner of Bayard and Mulberry for twenty minutes. The pain in her ankle screamed. The painful vibrations were dissolved by the steam that rises in thick, blue-gray columns from subterranean cavities where the city cages her oldest secrets so they won't asphyxiate the air. As aloneness and industriousness commingled in a cocktail of anxiety, Mrs. Zimmerman's desperation snowballed. She remembered the day Sasha, her attractive Polish au pair, had failed to collect her after a weekend ski vacation in Vermont. All the other children had gone home long ago, but Mrs. Zimmerman had sat on a log bench beneath a tacky fake stuffed moose head and waited, hungry and sad, for two hopeless hours. That ancient horror of abandonment threatened to be re-lived now, and she'd do anything to avoid it. She debated returning to the Shanghai Tea Parlor to ask to use their phone, but her children, her manicurist, and the caterer were the only numbers she had committed to memory.

Outside, the weather was still a furnace. It radiated at her. Three-thirty came—still no sign of Max. Mrs. Zimmerman dragged herself along Pell Street for no reason other than to evade despair. Slowly, she first picked her way, crossing the street to go along the shady side. But something grabbed her kitten heel from below before she could get there. Her foot plunged into a gap in the pavement, and she plummeted to the ground without any grace whatsoever. Countless nearby pedestrians witnessed this fall. None rushed to her aid. She scooped up her clutch and invested all her strength in standing up, smoothing her now-ruined dress, and not crumbling in front of TD Bank. Rather hyperbolically, she crawled toward the safety of the curb. No longer able to walk, Mrs. Zimmerman deposited her body on the nearest stoop.

Unbeknownst to Mrs. Zimmerman (for she was too preoccupied with her misery and the state of her dress to notice such things), the doorstep where she was now squatting was the very same one up which she had seen the old crone disappear into her apartment gleefully loaded with fresh fish and groceries. That same woman now watched Mrs. Zimmerman from the portcullis that served her tiny kitchen as a window. This White woman's hysteria was way more entertaining than anything currently playing on NY1. So, the old woman settled on a stool to watch the show while munching on pork gaifan and plucking freshly made baozi with chopsticks from a bamboo steamer.

Emotional compression knitted Mrs. Zimmerman's ribs together, causing her throat to close. The air around her face heated up with hateful tropical humidity. *Oh no no no no no no.* It was about to happen. She was about to be *that* woman who breaks down in plain view of all of New York City and just cries and cries. But then, the deus ex machina occurred.

Heavenly Hands: Qi Gong Tui Na, Chinese Massage: 15-minute foot massage, $15.

There was a sign—it was fate. Mrs. Zimmerman used her sleeve to pull open the door with a colorful foot meridian chart taped to it. It tinkled its bells at her as she hauled her body up the narrow staircase using one leg and two arms.

Heavenly Hands was not at all like the immaculate spas of Madison Avenue. It was not even sterile. Instead, it was some sort of massage factory, a dirty dark hole where men with sallow skin and small eyes traded on the flesh of exhausted White bodies spread out on paper-covered gurneys. It was a literal sweatshop, this long, skinny space. *How does the city not shut these places down?*

Through her shudders, she could see that the velvet hangings of the opium den had been taken outside for a shaking. A small cash register was propped up on a desk by a bay window beneath banners of cranes embroidered on red printed silk. Some sort of calendar? Behind it huddled four skinny Asians. The gender of at least one was unclear to Mrs. Zimmerman. Having lost some of her ancestors in the

Holocaust, she'd never been raised to airbrush entire populations and, somehow, did it anyway. She allowed the thought, *Well, they all look alike,* to enter her head without policing it. On a bench on the opposing wall sat four more, including one that rose to greet her.

The small, squinty Asian woman wore a blue Nike logo t-shirt and a servant's smirk. Her voice was weighted like an accusation.

"Can I help you, miss?"

When Mrs. Zimmerman was clearly a *ma'am,* the use of *miss* felt deliberately pejorative. Already, she resented this wretched mustard-skinned worker. Bad English flowed through her crooked gray teeth like toxic sludge in the Pearl River. The way she carried himself around Mrs. Zimmerman, all scrunched, made her feel as if economic growth came at a very high environmental cost.

Taken aback by this...let's call it cultural coldness... Mrs. Zimmerman took a minute to respond, for she was in a kind of awe state. Pain and curiosity had created a sense of possibility for her, which she hadn't touched on in years. For a moment, while she shocked herself into her new surroundings, basic presence dawned.

Voyeurism was removed from the voyeur. Lights dimmed, then tinted red. Oriental tinkling floated off unseen speakers and kind of relaxed her. It was less annoying than expected. In the back, cubbies long enough for a human to lie down in were cordoned off by plain shower curtains. The thin walls murmured with "oohs," "aahs," and "right there's." The incensed air was unrecycled and mustier than the back of a Pakistani's taxicab. Mrs. Zimmerman could feel the foreign molecules attacking her crepe de chine and lodging there. The Chinese dry cleaners on Park and 75th would get it out. There was no foulness they couldn't obliterate with their secret Oriental dry-cleaner magic. But until she scrubbed herself for an hour and dispatched Chloe with the dirties, the third-world scents would have to be carried on her clothes and hair.

Immense discomfort descended. Mrs. Zimmerman's curiosity was satisfied as it needed to be. Anxiously, she backpedaled toward the door. She was stopped by bumping into an ancient, boxy television blurrily looping clips filmed in the mid-90s of an attractive young Chinese woman demonstrating what Mrs. Zimmerman could only imagine were "tui na" techniques on a prone subject.

"Sorry," she murmured, more to the wobbling television than the woman in the chair beside it.

The squinty-faced woman stepped toward the television with one palm turned up. She swatted the TV, which promptly stopped swaying. Around her wrist was bound a thin, red thread. It was tied too tight, causing her flesh to pucker on either side. "TV always OK. Do not worry. So, nothing for you today then, miss?"

Mrs. Zimmerman's rebuttal was prepared. She was about to deliver it when a soft voice, almost feminine but belonging to a man, addressed her in flawed English.

"Please allow me do something about ankle, miss."

"Pardon me?"

"Pain. You must feel pain. A lot of pain."

Mrs. Zimmerman lowered her eyes before raising them again to meet those of the outspoken immigrant stranger. He was a young man in his late twenties (though with Asians, one can never really tell). He was Chinese, obviously, with straight black hair that fell just below his ears and dressed in a plain white t-shirt and outdated jeans. Nikes that were not new but still in meticulous condition and were on his feet. Mrs. Zimmerman met the man's gaze, and the oblong shape of the eyes began to change. *Is that a dragon flying across the irises?* The rest of the man's kin, colleagues, or whatever they were looking on in silent amusement.

"What's your name?" She hadn't intended to ask the question; it just asked itself.

"Mike."

At once, she felt relieved that she'd been given familiar syllables but also slightly hurt not to be presented with his elaborate Chinese name calligraphed on rice paper like a diplomat's gift.

"Nice to meet you, Mike. I'm Lauren."

She gave her first name without thinking. Or rather, it gave itself.

"Hi Lauren, I am obliged. Please, this way."

Mike gestured to one of the frightening cubicles down the parlor's gullet, and Lauren shrank without meaning to.

"It's OK, ma'am. We are very clean here. Promise. We change the shits every time."

"No, it's not that...." She felt ridiculous for what she was about to say, all the more so for saying it while clutching her lizard clutch with a Cartier watch strapped to her wrist. "It's that...I only have $17 on me right now."

The squinty-eyed woman next to the television chortled, then covered her mouth. Mike shot her fiery eyes, which shut her up so quickly that Lauren almost felt sorry for her.

"It's OK, miss. We take credit card. You do tip in cash."

Usually, she would have walked out and immediately left a very opinionated anonymous Yelp review. But Mike smiled a little at her without blushing, which made her blush. Why was she trying to entangle her fantasizing faculties with a foreign low-wage worker barely older than her son? It wasn't sexual, but it *was* something.

"You have bad injury that only get worse if you ignore. Hands can help. You pay what you can and tip me nice next time, OK? This way, please."

"Alright. What's the harm? You seem very nice, and my ankle does hurt. It would be nice to sit for a minute. I'll just do 15 minutes, please."

As she followed Mike into the back, she blocked out the sounds of ecstasy oozing through the walls. She internally berated herself for urges that Stephen described as her "misguided philanthropic compulsions." He'd complain (and she'd agree) that "those who have less take pity on those who have more, and the whole thing makes everyone feel ashamed and wretched. Next time, sweetie, let me write the checks."

"Please."

Mike pulled back the shower curtain to reveal a tidy but sparse spa bivouac. She entered, and then he withdrew, indicating the little plastic hook where she could hang her current season designer look. She took off all her jewelry, including her wedding band and Cartier watch, and sealed them inside the liner pocket of her clutch. Lauren undressed with halting fingers, as one does at the doctor's when the doctor's sex and age may feel predatory to the patient. There was also something thrilling about undressing in what was, for her, practically *plein air*. She stood naked, without her wedding band. Something she never did unless she was in the shower or praying for the lovemaking to be over, though she dared not look at herself.

Lauren eased her body gently onto the massage table. Her hot skin recoiled at the first touch of the cool surface. She climbed the rest of the way on, and relief came at once, waltzing in as soon as the weight was removed from her ankle. As she forced her cheeks into the paper-covered cradle, all thoughts of self-condemnation or the Bill and Melinda Gates Fund immediately evaporated. Now that a long sheet of paper was all that separated her naked body from a table that had borne the tired limbs of Manhattan's masses, all she could think was *sweating, grunting, and surreptitious hard-ons.*

Mike returned. He pretended to knock on the shower curtain.

"Ready?"

No. But she called out anyway, "Yes!"

The Asian man pattered into the room. He had a distinct way of walking in his soft-soled Nikes. She'd already memorized it.

"Lay still, miss. Receive the qi."

Before she could ask what the hell "key" was, warmth was all around her in the form of a hot bath sheet.

The paper crackled beneath her body every time she moved. The foot attached to her inflamed ankle was now nestled in Mike's strong hands. Ripples of energy, feeling, and pain ran suddenly through invisible channels in her body, channels she'd never even known were there. Mike's fingers were soft and warm as they clasped the injured ankle and rubbed the ball of her foot. The whole of the lower leg and foot was now being wrapped and compressed inside a cold towel, now hot, now cold again. His touch was euphoria, and her parched limbs rose eagerly to immerse themselves in this unknown but gentle oasis. Pleasurable probes were savored equally with the pain while Mike pushed around the pins and needles in her ankle. He wheeled on, and powerful aromas started wafting into the room—cinnamon, peppermint, red pepper.

The belly of Mike's thumb pressed into the ball of Lauren's left foot, then broadened the movement to encompass the whole of her upper toe ridge with his palm. Gradually, he increased force, slowly causing a kind of exquisite distending sensation to radiate. It spread up her leg and filled her belly before spreading across her chest. Though the pain was sharp, she could feel something loosening as Mike carefully kneaded the pincushion of flesh enclosing her ankle's joint. His twig-like fingers honed in on specific, tender points. When he would strike one, Lauren would let out an inadvertent hiss of air before drawing back sharply inwards. Only then did relief follow, rushing over her like a wave crashing with intense color explosions. Green, now red, now yellow, and blue washed over the backs of her sealed eyelids. Stagnant blood woke up and dissipated from her ankle. The fluid in her foot began to dislodge and oxygenate upward, with Mike's hands following right along. He squeezed her calves with his thumb and index finger before clasping the whole of his hand upon her knees and twiddling quickly and powerfully. His strong hands ran up and down the length of her left leg, fingers intertwining and interlocking. At one point, she felt him tracing her taut scapular muscles with smooth, hot stones.

An instrumental version of a 90s pop song was playing in the background. She'd always hated that peppy, unnaturally optimistic tune. But confined to a duet between a piano and flute, she enjoyed the melody and surrendered her body to its notes. The momentary paralysis of pure relaxation, where the body becomes a safe harbor in which the mind lightly anchors, took over. Physiologically speaking, it was the best massage she'd ever had (and she'd had every massage *Conde Nast Traveler* decided was worth mentioning). His touch was intimate. It was not like a lover's, but like a lover in that love was there. There was gentleness, and there was warmth. *Perhaps those two things have something in common. Something to do with what aging hippies and divorced yoginis refer to as "self-healing."*

Mike handled Lauren's body and wounded ankle like priceless porcelain. Or an ancient manuscript. Or his child. Or beloved. But no, she was precious to him simply because she was in a body that was alive. And that was it. Plain life, extraordinary life. Even his hands were velvety smooth. Nobody had put their fingers on her like this before, not that she could remember.

Had touch ever not been performative comfort before? She reached for him with her thoughts but was not received.

Again, Mike slipped unnoticed from the cubicle to fetch another warm towel or hot stone. Aware that the walls were only fabric, Lauren suddenly thought about who was lying on either side of her body, halfway to his happy ending. She found herself wondering if happy endings were real. Between Mike's soft footsteps padding back toward her, she heard a swish and a groan that made her recoil. Somehow, her fifteen minutes had turned into an eternity of bliss.

Lauren didn't want to get off that table.

"Miss, our time finish. Please wake up."

Lauren returned to her body half-entranced. It was already after four o'clock. He'd massaged her for an hour. The pain in her ankle remained, but it was bearable. The lemon-toned kitten heels lay innocently on the floor beneath a plastic chair. Her fingertips grazed the delicate straps with dismay, and the work of making herself presentable began anew.

When she was buttoned but still barefoot, Mike reappeared. Had he been watching her, bathed naked in broken neons, all this time? In his hands were a Dixie cup of room temperature water and a humble pair of hot pink, plastic mesh Chinese slippers covered in hideous beads. He smiled and held them out respectfully. Instead of being repulsed, Lauren was relieved.

"You cannot wear high heel for at least one month, OK?"

Lauren nodded, slid on the hideous shippers, and drifted into the lobby area. She tried to explain in front of the women about the money for the extra time, but Mike put his hands in front of his face and waved them.

"No, no, no. And miss, you be careful. Love not supposed to be this way."

A lingering warmth, qi or whatever they called it, was still on her when she exited the little massage parlor on Pell. She thought of Max. How nice would it be to skip the standing appointment with Stephen and just drive around the island for a while?

"Take me somewhere I've never been," she'd say, delighting in the widening of his surprised eyes. "Like Flushing. Yes. Let's go to Flushing and have soup dumplings for dinner."

The familiar town car was parked on the corner of Baxter and Mulberry. A silhouetted figure that was definitely not Max idled in the driver's seat, totally absorbed in his phone. Lauren took faltering steps toward the town car but quickened her pace when the driver did not get out and open the door. The distinctly unfriendly sound of the vehicle being unlocked from within was heard. She yanked open the door and got in.

There was no point in asking about Max. She knew what had happened; she was just surprised it had happened so fast. Had her friends even bothered to wait until they were back uptown to phone their husbands (who then called *her* husband)?

"Welcome back, Arturo," she said coldly.

Arturo did not turn around, but she could see the white-hot flash of his grin in the rearview. "Always a pleasure to see you again, Mrs. Zimmerman. I hope you had a nice, er, treatment. Home, I presume?"

"Do I have a choice?"

The luxury vehicle pulled away from the modest Chinese storefront, driving until it rejoined Bowery, then followed 3rd Avenue all the way back uptown until it regained its title of Lexington Avenue.

Mrs. Zimmerman sorrowed silently in the cushioned leather backseat. Arturo's reappearance was her husband's proxy warfare. How had Stephen found out about her day? Why did he care?

Arturo pulled up outside the familiar aubergine canopy draped over the Zimmermans' particular piece of Park Avenue. He tipped his hat and grinned. "Have a nice evening, ma'am."

Despite stepping out into tropical swelter raging outside the air-conditioned vehicle, the warmth that had just suffused her, the qi or whatever, which she'd hoped she'd internalized, was gone. But so, too, was most of the pain in her ankle. Relief had taken its place, leaving her feeling like a stranger in her own home. It was five o'clock, but Stephen, of course, had yet to appear.

Into the steam shower, she went. She stripped off her cream satin dress, entered the thicket of perfumed fog, and stood there with the water swirling all around. She emerged but did not immediately obscure her nakedness in its oatmeal-colored cashmere robe. She sat on her towel at the foot of the California King for at least ten minutes and watched her flesh sag in the mirror. It was the first time since the children were born that she'd looked at herself deliberately without a surgeon present. She forgave herself as best she could before entombing herself in the walk-in and reemerging in a black silk top and pressed slacks. She had bought both pieces on a feeling and had never worn either.

The silk brushed sensuously against her skin, almost with the playful lightness of a lover's touch. It made her think of space; ancient, underground caverns; and the dark deeds done to her relatives by Nazis with the Big Dipper hanging over them. This soft darkness almost made her think of her mother. With great caution, Mrs. Zimmerman applied her makeup and dried her hair.

Then, she returned to the sitting room and adjusted a few art books, which were out of place on the shelves. Then, she rang for Chloe, who promptly fetched her some hibiscus team, which she sipped slowly while waiting for her husband to come home.

By Anonymous

HE NEEDED NO AGENT. The idea of art school made him belly laugh, and the subway reigned as his preferred gallery, for it was like Heraclitus's river, a ceaseless flow of subterranean change. The 4/5/6, the 1/2/3, the Q, the R, the A/C/E. For years, he'd been showing at them all.

Those who knew him best described him as "monkish." He always dressed the same. In a world exploding with personal expression, banality seemed to him "real" style, selfsame with renunciation. A white T-shirt, sky-blue windbreaker, jeans, and white tennis shoes—he owned multiples of each, all topped off with a sun-faded Yankees cap.

Even though it was irrelevant, he had a name. Two, in fact. Both discarded long ago. There was the one his grandparents had addressed him by in the land where his mother had given him life before losing her own. This one belonged only to the governments now—it had not been uttered in his presence in over forty years. The other was decreed unto him by a well-meaning family friend cosplaying as his "aunty," who'd pantomimed Ellis Island when he'd arrived in Jamaica Bay. With its familiar, easy-to-pronounce Anglican syllables, he gave this name to police, frazzled baristas to misspell, and Amazon deliveries. But in his day-to-day existence—the creative and the mundane—with no wife, children, or living relatives to answer to, he did not need the pretension of a name. Anonymity was far more elegant. Anonymous was a great name, like Anonymous Bosch. Most people, however, didn't ask. They took pictures of him and his work without permission and called him "that Asian subway artist with the broken thumb." As an epithet, he didn't hate it.

His medium was neither spray paint nor banjo nor random passenger portraits. Most of his customers called what he did "minimalist," "Zen-like," and "postmodern calligraphy." Though this was inaccurate (nothing he created was writing), correcting them took too much effort and implied that he had some sort of destination for his work. He was not on social media and was proud of it. The other subway artists, all prepubescent Harings, insisted it was the "only way to get noticed, like really noticed."

But those peers, followers of footsteps, existed as aliens to him. Their vision, their brands, and their scalability repulsed him. Though he'd never dare to say what was and what was not "pure" art, he never wanted to operate as a creator "in the style of." He was just a man who, at some point, while bored in his youth, had found a marker and moved it across some paper.

Becoming an artist for him was as natural as a waterfall. What else could he have done with his undocumented life, limited as it was by status and language? Laundry? Construction? Food delivery? Marriage to a White person with a blue passport? The expected lines of labor stretched forward and backward in time, according to the Western notion of progress. But time was not linear. His mother had died so that he might live until he died, forming a closed loop from which there was no escape. Except, perhaps, when making art.

Whomsoever appreciated his art, therefore, was doing so in the present moment. The people who were touched or intrigued without understanding why or needing to. These rare souls, not coveted collectors, were the buyers he sought. New York was always now; his task was to capture this understanding and concretize its expression so that others might also experience it. That was why he'd developed the "system."

About twenty years ago, he'd overheard a group of NYU girls getting on at West 4th prattling breathlessly about Charlotte's conversion to Judaism to marry Harry on *Sex and the City*. He'd never seen the show and didn't even own a TV, but their discussion of the rabbi's refusal of the well-intentioned heroine intrigued him.

"Do you think that's true?" asked one of the girls after explaining she was falling for a Jewish boy. "Do they really turn you away three times before letting you in?"

Since then, it had been Anonymous's policy to put potential patrons through their paces before selling anything. "Art in everyday life," he called his philosophy. Before anyone could take home his work, they'd have to find and beseech him—three times. His work deserved this, and so did the people. The process could (and did) take months if not years. Often, it was like the bridge to nowhere in the San Gabriel Mountains. The people came, took his card out of sympathy or curiosity, then turned the other way when they saw him again at some station or other months later. On those rare occasions when the philosophy was allowed to flow to its fruition, the result was the transfer of his work into the stewardship of someone who *really* wanted it.

Here's how it worked. During the first encounter, when the desire for ownership was initially broached, a would-be patron would pay him four dollars for his business card. Anonymous considered these cards micro-works of art in themselves, for he cut each one himself, late at night, squatting on the lone stool in his cramped galley kitchen. Approximate squares, they resembled the Midwestern states when seen from an airplane. Unmarked by writing or numbers, they bore only his seal, which consisted of an impression of his crooked thumb in strawberry-colored ink. Its elongated oval shape reminded him of an elliptical planetary nebulae he'd seen at a New Year's Day show at the Hayden Planetarium. Except, instead of closed spheres, his nebulae were open systems. While some might demean the shape as a "smear," the discerning eye saw a break in the shape trailing off on one side into infinity, like a comet's tail.

If a serious card carrier found him again, they would present Anonymous with his own card and eight dollars exact (even when he could make change, he refused). Only then would Anonymous take back the smaller card and hand the client a larger one in exchange. About the size of an index card, again hand cut, again sealed with his thumbprint. If they agreed to step two, he'd write the name of the work (or works) they were interested in buying on this card, then, again, send them away. Should they find him a third time and produce the index card, he would sell them the works listed at whatever price they felt was fair to pay for it. He never told his clients where or when he would they could find him.

Many remarked on his ability to draw such straight lines with a crooked thumb. Once, NY1 had offered to feature him on their "Stoop Chat" segment. (He refused.)

"How do you hold the brush or pen so steady?" the reporter had wanted to know.

His right thumb was actually perfectly whole. Not one metacarpal bone had ever been broken. Bequeathed unto him at birth, his finger's fish-hook shape was a deformity known as Dupuytren's contracture. He liked to imagine it as a souvenir from the man who'd impregnated his mother. The painless result of tissue knots tied together under the skin to form a thick cord, these unseen biological ties pulled the finger into its bent position. There would only be pain if he chose to have them surgically severed to straighten the bones out. He'd never considered it the way most healthily sighted people never considered a cornea transplant. His thumb was the pilot of his right hand. The maker of the "first dot" of every one of his works and the strawberry-red seal in the lower right-hand corner of each work, which served as their "eyes."

Instead of dismissing the reporter, he should have confessed and let her broadcast the truth: "My thumb is my earthly emissary of basic beauty. It's what makes me an artist."

One October day, after lunch but before the end of the workday, the 51st Street Station was exceptionally peaceful. Everyone who worked in the massive corporate buildings glued their hips to their desks, making money. St. Patrick's Cathedral was closed to clean the sea-blue stained glass in the Lady Chapel, which redirected the tourists some fifty-odd blocks north to photograph St. John the Divine.

Anonymous arrived after the morning rush. He began the day as usual by meticulously arranging his works, enshrined in cheap frames from a dollar store in Yonkers, on a canvas drop cloth. All lined up in the lower righthand corners, the strawberry-colored seals permeated a sense of order.

A thirty-something man in pencil jeans and red-framed glasses with his hair tied off to resemble ebi nigiri stood with his jacket draped over one shoulder between the stairs and the platform. He clutched a glossy black Phillips-branded folder and stared without speaking at Anonymous's drop cloth. Anonymous could tell that the man was waiting to be addressed and took pleasure in denying him the satisfaction. A second of silence stretched into a minute, then two. Finally, the well-dressed voyeur with so many better places to be cleared his throat.

"Hey, man. These are surprisingly good. How much do they go for?"

"Not for sale."

"Excuse me you?"

"Not for sale for you today. You take my card. You find me again. Then, maybe, I sell you something."

The man rolled his eyes. He accepted the artist's card and offered him one in return.

"Whatever, man. Don't you think you're a little old for the whole obscurity, scarcity, and thumbing the nose at the whole system thing? Whatever. If you change your mind, give me a call."

Jake M. Dexter

Strange New World Gallery

108 W. 18th Street

Anonymous shrugged. He threw the card onto the train tracks just as the incoming train screamed into the station.

In March, on a cold but clear Sunday in Union Square, Anonymous watched a girl die. She looked either Korean or Japanese. She was young and not considered beautiful for an Asian by Western standards, but her features would have been appreciated back home.

He lied to the police, "No, officer. I did not see anyone push her. I did not hear a scream, just the sound of yellow flowers falling."

In April, the man with the ebi bun and the red glasses returned. Well, it was more like the city had finally recycled him back around. To Anonymous's surprise, he produced the card he had given him back in October.

"You never called."

Anonymous shrugged.

"Well, lucky for you, I finally found you again. Listen, I've just signed on for some funding to showcase undiscovered immigrant artists. I get that you're anti-everything. Everything, probably, except money."

The opening occurred at the end of July when all the important patrons and real artists were off in places like the South of France or the Hamptons. White wine went round on circular trays clutched in the fingers of attractive blond and black-haired young people of every and no gender. Reporters and collectors circumambulated. One, who looked like a cross between a biker chick and a librarian, pointed her phone at Anonymous and began recording.

"I'm here at the opening of the longtime subway artist known as Anonymous, who the illustrious Jacob Dexter at Strange New World Gallery on West 18th recently discovered. With the recent rise in violence against Asians, the exhibition is perfectly timed to shine a light on these voices. The name of the show is 'Subway: A Visual Haiku.' Your ink works are highly abstract. Lots of brush calligraphic references, Zen colors, and reinterpreted ensōs. Tell me, Mister Anonymous, what do they symbolize?"

"Nothing. They are symbols of themselves."

There were red dots on every single work. Except one. Mr. Dexter was doing math in his head and grinning.

The last guests trickled out. The caterers gathered up their napkins and plastic wine cups, then whisked all evidence of the event away. White walls covered in Anonymous's works closed him in on all sides. It wasn't nihilistic, but the experience felt void—like the best possible version of the afterlife he could imagine.

"Hell yes, man. Sold every painting except one. We crushed it tonight!"

Jake held up his palm for a high five, but Anonymous did not twitch a finger.

"Alright, man, whatever. You need to give me your bank details so I can get you paid."

Anonymous shook his head. He pointed with his crooked thumb to the unsold painting.

"Just give that one back. You donate rest to the city."

"Are you sure, man? These funds can change your life."

"Life doesn't need to be changed."

The artist declined the cab offered by the gallerist. Even though he spent most of his days sitting at subway stations, he never actually rode the trains. Walking through his city, especially at strange, shoulder hours, was his kinhin. He loved bathing in the forest of buildings glowing with yellow rectangles of light. He walked at a consistent pace with the unsold work tucked between his elbow and ribcage, stopping only at red (never yellow) lights. As he reached the Museum of Natural History, it began to rain. Recent protests had succeeded in prodding the city to relocate the bronze of Theodore Roosevelt on horseback flanked by two shirtless, unnamed men of indigenous and African descent to North Dakota. Where the president had lorded over the steps for some four score years, now only white scaffolding trimmed with a black tarp rustled in the wind. Anonymous whisked off his Yankees cap, allowing the raindrops to baptize his brow, and bowed low to the vacant plinth.

It took Anonymous three hours to reach his small but light-filled two-bedroom in the Heights where Adam, his longtime partner, was waiting. Adam folded Anonymous into his arms as soon as he crossed the door. On the coffee table, their favorite tea and bedtime snack of dried prunes were waiting.

"I'm so proud of you, my beloved. Are you the toast of town?"

Despite what the press release professed, Anonymous had never been homeless.

A few days later, before the commuters began their commute, Anonymous rolled his shopping trolley to the 181st Street A Station. The cheaply framed works arranged carefully inside were not newer than those hanging in the gallery in another galaxy downtown, just better.

Only the bodega and the corner produce stand were open. The men who ran them greeted the artist familiarly as he went by. Anonymous tipped his Yankees cap, as he always did, out of respect for the understanding that these men (along with taxi drivers and home health aides) were the only people in the city who worked harder than he did. The hours and their emptiness, not their backgrounds or professions, connected them.

Anonymous sipped scalding hot black tea in residence on the platform. He nibbled on a warm banana produced from his pocket, humming an old Beach Boys tune. He unrolled the soft, many times washed canvas drop cloth, then laid out the frames, one by one. There was no order to his arrangement, and yet there was. All his favorite works flowed together in a narrative that would make sense to anyone who bothered to look.

The strawberry-red seals of his elliptical thumbprint were all lined up in the bottom right-hand corner of each work. While the brushwork was always the immediate focus, the seals, neither too close nor too far from the strokes or the pages' abyss, were responsible for the pieces' unity.

The commuters arrived. The women wore sneakers or comfortable sandals while high-heels peeked from the canvas totes slung over their shoulders. The men abstained from ties and loosened their top buttons to keep sweat from polluting their collars. Children released from school for weeks now swung their legs back and forth in their strollers, passing a chosen toy through their fingers. Nannies wiped the sweat from their brows while teenagers in ripped denim shorts huddled and chattered about their friends' lives with the utmost importance. An anonymous hundred and then another anonymous hundred floated by, and the artist was invisible to them all.

The morning rush finally tapered, like a raging mountain river the farther it gets from spring. A dark-haired woman in her late twenties dressed in colorful prints carrying a quart of strawberries from the fruit cart on the corner stopped at the edge of his drop cloth and peered around. The little crimson heap contained by the pulpous walls of forest green made him smile. *What a lovely fruit sculpture.* She pointed first to the works, then to him.

"Hey … I know you. I know this work. I'm pretty sure I saw them on Instagram the other day. You're that new Thai artist showing at the Strange New World Gallery, no?"

The artist did not answer. He just gestured to the works.

"What's your name?"

He waved his hands back and forth as if clearing a path for gnats. She picked up the one from the gallery that hadn't sold. The girl of a similar age who'd filmed him at the gallery had described it as a "reinterpreted ensō." Though none of his works "depicted" anything, Anonymous was particularly fond of that one because, for no reason, it reminded him of his childhood dog's paws flying through the grass.

"I don't know why, but I love this one. It reminds me of something, but I'm not sure what. How much?"

"Not for sale for you today. You take my card. You find me again. Then, maybe, I sell you something."

The young woman frowned.

"That's ridiculous. You know I can just go down to Chelsea and buy whatever I want of yours right now, right? Well, I mean, I could if I had the money, which I don't. I'm an artist too, you know. And if I were you, and I'd showed at a major Chelsea gallery, I wouldn't persist in my pretention and continue to loaf around subway stations like some sort of undiscovered genius." Her hand suddenly flew to her mouth. "Oh my god! I didn't mean just to say all of that out loud. I'm *so* sorry. I didn't mean to offend. But hey, what about this? What if I trade you these strawberries for the painting? Like as a down payment. Then, maybe, one day, when I make it, you come find me, and I'll repay the rest by giving you one of my works."

Anonymous raised an eyebrow. No one had ever spoken so directly to him before. He'd been berated at a distance many more times than he'd ever made love. But for fear of triggering homeless man hysteria, these confrontations never occurred within arm's reach.

The woman's youthful assurance blazed. Her dreams for the future were full of fire. For some reason that he couldn't place, she reminded him of his mother. What she might have been like had she lived and not died giving birth to him all those years ago. Given the girl's personality, he imagined her work wasn't outstanding. However, a fruit sculpture for a painting was an intriguing proposition. Her earnestness and hunger for art and all its creative and commercial largesse charmed him. It did and did not signal appreciation for the moment.

He slowly picked up the work in question.

"OK, Ms. Artist Lady. We have a deal."

Acknowledgments

Special thanks to Sabina Kencana for her fantastic cover design; Manuel Quintana for his expert and elegant work on the interior layout; Emma Moylan for her eagle-eyed edit; my AAPI and NYC crews, who shared their truths with me; and Poodle, Bert, Kei, Lindsay, Joel, and Bill Birns for always reading and believing.

ERIKA TANAKA is a native New Yorker who writes short fiction and essays. She is also the author of the novella *East Village Wabi Sabi*.

www.ingramcontent.com/pod-product-compliance
Lightning Source LLC
Chambersburg PA
CBHW030109260626
47156CB00008B/2593